MADAM FATE

MADAM FATE

Marcia Douglas

SOHO

Published by

Soho Press, Inc.
853 Broadway
New York NY 10003

Library of Congress Cataloging-in-Publication Data

Douglas, Marcia, 1961-
    Madam Fate / Marcia Douglas.
        p.   cm.
    ISBN 1-56947-134-7 (alk. paper)
    I. Title.
PS3554.08274m3   1999
813' .54--dc21   98-20395
                                                      CIP

10 9 8 7 6 5 4 3 2 1

For my mother

Acknowledgments

The completion of this project was made possible by the Clifford Clark Fellowship Foundation at State University of New York, Binghamton. Special thanks goes to Barry Targan, Carole Boyce Davies, Isidore Okpewho, and Sidonie Smith.

I also wish to acknowledge all the friends and colleagues who have encouraged and supported my work, including teachers at the Ohio State University Creative Writing Program and Sylvia Barnes at Oakwood College.

I am indebted to my parents, Bernice and Leo Douglas, for their strength; to my brother Leo, and my sisters Carol, Bev, Gem, and Ena for their love; to Laurent for being there—merci; to Laura Hruska for her hard work; and to the ancestors for their laughter.

Moon marked and touched by sun
my magic is unwritten
but when the sea turns back
it will leave my shape behind.

—Audre Lorde, "A Woman Speaks"

Contents

In the Beginning

In the Beginning: Xaymaca—Jamaica

IN THE BEGINNING, THERE WAS laughter. God was lying down at the bottom of the sea, taking an afternoon nap—her plaits set in motion by the rhythm of warm water, seaweed brushing against her skin. She was minding her own business as God often does; her arms circled her stomach and she dreamed of giving birth to a child who would be born laughing. In this dream, the baby gasped for air and then burst into laughter so loud and so long that the midwife had to slap its little bottom to make it stop. The baby stopped for a while, then took one look at the midwife and began laughing again. Its laughter was so contagious that soon everyone was doubling over and wiping tears from their eyes.

This is a story my Mama, Anna, used to tell. Mama said a long time ago, before this island even had a name, before it was called Jamaica, and even before it was called Xaymaca, God used to take a nap in the warm waters here.

One day God was in the middle of this favorite dream; she had a little smile on her face as fish nibbled at her navel when suddenly she was interrupted by a vision of the future. Now everyone knows that evil travels in straight lines, so when God saw the future billowing toward her straight as a fleet of ships, she became afraid because she saw that these ships were filled with sorrow. On board there was screaming and moaning, and the sea was thick with blood; God saw and heard it all and anger burned red hot in her womb; she howled and rumbled under the sea but all the oceans put together could not contain her wrath. She opened her mouth and the ocean floor buckled, then shutting her eyes tight, she folded over and heaved. God heaved and heaved, the ocean floor trembled, and she spewed out fire—orange-yellow flames and hot lava everywhere. This, said my Mama, is the story of how our archipelago was born.

My Mama said that suddenly in the middle of all this, God, as if remembering a secret, stopped. She squinted her eyes and looked way past the future billowing toward her, past the sea of blood and its red horizon, to dark figures rising in the distance, walking on the water. What God saw was her daughter and her daughter's daughters, and she threw back her head and laughed right out loud. God's laughter spun around and around; it reverberated over the earth, and under the waters which covered the earth. It spiraled up and down and back again. God laughed such a belly-laugh so loud and so long that the laughter seeped into the hot lava, effervescing and churning, cooling to form the land under our feet.

Centuries have passed, ships have come and gone, and to this day, if you put your head to the ground, you can still hear God's laughter. Lizards hear this laughter, and so do dragonflies and butterflies, and my Mama said all the women on this island are connected by the laughter like beads on a string; our laughter makes us unstoppable. Mama gave me two bits of advice, she said: Remember your laughter, and when you eat guava, don't swallow the seeds because they might take root and grow in you . . .

In the beginning there was laughter, but to hear a woman's laughter one must first hear her sorrow . . .

Her sorrow/my sorrow, my poison arrow, my heart-pain, my troubled thing, how can I tell it? Let's call me Bella. I am also the woman people call kin-owl, that woman who lives in her flesh by day, then takes off her skin, living in spirit by night. A kin-owl must always keep her true identity secret; she must never reveal who she really is. She could be the woman who sells you the morning paper, or the one you see waiting at the bus stop for a ride into town; she could be your neighbor or your best friend, your very flesh and blood—your mother or sister or first-born—but you would never know. Let's call me Bella. People fear a woman who shifts shape (how many people would feel comfortable knowing that their neighbor sheds her skin at night?), so a woman like me keeps her secret to protect others. Nevertheless, secrets are difficult to bear—there are moments when the soul longs for exposure. There are words which beg to be expelled from the chest. This is my challenge: how to tell my story while keeping my identity secret. I am young and I am old; I am flesh and I am spirit, the beginning and the never-ending. In the beginning there was laughter but inside the laughter was so much sorrow. Sorrow has bloated and filled me up. My insides are puffy, my tummy swollen like a watermelon. This is an angry sorrow. A sorrow that wants to be free, that demands to be told. But to whom can I tell it?

There is a woman, Ida, whom the spirits love. She once heard God laugh, then men in white jackets came and locked her in a mental institution. Ida is a good listener. Sometimes at night she hears my moaning but even she doesn't know who I really am. She sits out in the asylum-sun all day talking to the washer women or the food service workers or the young volunteers or the other patients—teaching them to listen, she says.

Perhaps she will teach me to lean closer to the ground, to grow my ears long and remember God's laughter.

• Part One •

Periwinkle

Ida

Excerpt from *The Long-Ears Woman's Book of Herbs*

Periwinkle (Catharanthus roseus)
Common Names: Old Maid, Ram Goat Roses, Brown Man's Fancy
Other Names: 'Winkles, Brown Girl's Forget-me-not
Drunk as a tea, this flowering plant is an excellent cure for diarrhea, toothache, nerves and other ailments. When admired as a garden flower, its blossoms become long-lasting, long-remembering, true-true friends.

One

PEOPLE ASK WHY I walk with a limp. Well, from when my eyes was at my knee, somehow I always felt lopside. I was born with nine fingers, you know, the little finger on my right hand missing, and in all the picture them, my left nostril always seem little higher than the other one, like the raise eyebrow on that side lifting it up. Nowadays I carry my rain pan in my right arm and the weight on that side seem to even things out a bit. Then at times I hold my head a certain kinda way just so the place a little tilt and everything seem alright. This, mind you, make some people wonder whether the lopside is really something wrong with my head, but let me leave that for them to figure out . . . Young Miss? Miss-Hanging-the-Towels, you say you just felt rain?

There is something about rain that soothes me—the sound pitter-pat, pat-pat, over and over. Pitter-pat, pat-pat. Mmm. This whole rain business is a funny-funny thing. You know, there's a woman here in the Garden, Mimi, who they say been drive crazy by the sound of water dripping in her head. One drop, plop, dripping from way up the top of her skull and then all the way down to some deep-deep water hole behind her tongue. Sake of this everlasting dripping, she can't even hardly speak, her tongue tie, every time the water make plop, she have to gasp and catch her breath, "Hup." So she always sound like she have hiccups. Lord, you should hear her. She write on a piece of brown paper bag, telling me say the dripping behind her tongue remind her of drought—like when the water barrel run low, and the grass all quail-up, and all you can get outta the stand-pipe is just a little drip drip drip, and all you can get outta the green water coconut after it done share around for everybody is just enough to barely wet your tongue. What a thing, eh? Every mawga dog and black puss have her own story, I tell you. So listen to this, I think I can help her—I know how to make it rain, you know.

The other thing I enjoy is the whisper in seashell and dry coconut husk. If you put these to your ear, you hear whoosh, whoosh, whoosh, like someone calling real soft from way back, or way forward. Whoosh, whoosh, whoosh. I am a listener, you know. I listen to rain; I listen to voices calling and I listen to all these animals and plants you see run-ning around here. But let me tell you this, in all my listening (and I've done quite a bit), the voice that grab my heart-ears the most is the one I found waiting for me right inside of a dry calabash. Put that husk to your ear, and ahh, you will hear some things that will bring you to repentance. I keep my calabash pot in a small basket that I always carry around with me; and let me tell you, this calabash is special-special. I use a pen-knife to cut out the sides with a lizard smiling from around rocks and leaves and things. People say lizards bring bad luck, but that's only because they fraid that the news the lizard brings might not be what they want hear. I keep the other half of the same calabash tuck up in my brassiere; for one thing it's safe there, close to my heart, and con-venient, and for another, I only have one breast and so the half-a-cal-abash in my bra make me look like I have two. Whoosh, whoosh, whoosh—songs of the forgotten dead, that's what that sound is. But you have to be careful who you tell these things to, sister-chile, because when you is a listener, and you understand these voice, and talk about them, people think you mad, and they put you away in places just like this. You try to explain to them what you hear, but of course they just take you for a fool because they don't really listen you. You know what I mean? Which remind me of another thing: By the time I finish hav-ing my say with you (yes, you over there, yes, you with the pink apron), you will know how to *listen*, and you will be a long-ears woman, just like me. Oh yes, I'll see to it.

That's the problem with young people nowadays, you know, they don't take the time to listen. Just be still. Take your mind in your two hands, and steal away. Listen for the place far-far behind the clanking pots them in the kitchen. Drink a little ceracee tea. Wait for the voices them. Trust me, as God be my judge, they are there. I hear them myself. Shhh. Hush, chile.

I was born during rainy time. The rain was just carrying on like mad that night, batta-batta, batta-batta, all over the little zinc roof. I could hear it clear-clear, beating on the breadfruit tree leaf them, beating gainst the window them, beating on the concrete floor on the verandah, then beating gainst the front door, and I knew it was time for me to just come on out and be born. I was born right inna Mother Duncan two big ole hand. There was a presence in the room, something trying to stop me from breathing—I feel it like a big ole paw trying to crush my lungs, but because I was determine to live and live and live, I open my mouth and I holler with all my might. My mother, she smile like a please-puss then, and the rain hold off to a drizzle, and for a while all was peace in the little room till Mother Duncan, with her long trumpet-mouth, announce, "Lord God-a-mighty, the chile only have nine fingers!" This was around 1920 (give or take a little) and I don't know how it is now, but back then, a child with nine fingers was not a good sign. Mother Duncan bathe me in a little lukewarm water, take my navel string, wrap it up in a white cloth, and leave it for my mother to bury under the poinciana tree in the yard. She did want to leave the house quick-quick, a nine-finger child was a bad omen, and she had better be gone. The rain was still falling soft when she leave; I hear the front door swing, bam, and she disappear in the rain drops.

My mother, Selma, did young and feeble, and she sick for seven days; she feed me her little thin milk, but she whoop and she cough, and she whoop and she cough and wasn't able to even step foot outside. Papa help much as he could. He was blind as a rat-bat from birth, you know,

but the two of them make a living weaving straw and carving wood
spoon for Mama to sell in the market with her sweetie and seasoning
and thing. That night, he hobble around trying to draw little ginger tea,
changing the diapers Mama make from flour bag, singing a little sing-
song, and all the while it rain and rain and Mama whoop and cough.
Meanwhile, the navel string stay same place on the windowsill where
Mother Duncan leave it, till when it begin to rot and stink, Papa find it
and plant it best as he could, the poor soul, under a calabash tree.

Now everybody know that a gourdie tree draw spirit, so when word
get around the district that Miss Selma nine-finger baby navel string
was bury (misbury, mind you) under a duppie tree, Lord have mercy,
tongues start to fly from church pew to chamber pot. Mama and Papa,
God bless their souls, try to make light of it, but the story follow me all
the way to school, the children laughing after me, mocking me and calling me "nine-finger duppie." School-pickney and wickedness—what a
tribulation!

(Speaking of which, this nurse that they have walking around the
ward is up to no good, I tell you. Look at her over there by the medicine
tray with her two-horn white hat, one end pointing west, the other
pointing east. A divided soul, that's what she is. Every time I hear her
white-polish shoes squeaking on the concrete, I have to turn my head
and listen to something else, the everlasting squeak-squeak, enough to
put my teeth on edge. You try to tell Nurse Watson the truth of things
but she can't hear you—her ears all stop up with only-God-knows-what.
Plenty times I try to make her understand that I am not mad and I am
not fool, but she just look through me like I'm not even here. I make it
as far as fifth-book, you know. You see me here in this Garden, but I seen
things and been places she don't even know how to dream bout, and
when I ready I can speak hoity-toity just like her. These people learn a
few fancy words and learn how to speak up in their nose, and straight
away they believe they have it over you, but they can't even tell head
from tail.)

But, as I was saying, as the nine-finger duppie, it was easy for me to
just keep quiet in a corner hoping they would forget me. You know

what I mean? And the funny thing is, it was round about that time that I start to listen, and I start to hear things. Now across the hill from where we were living was what they used to call a rolling calf race-course. People used to walk and make a wide circle around this spot so as to avoid meeting up with the rolling calf, and sometime in the dead o' night you could hear his chain dragging, dragging, dragging behind him all restless-like on the ground. I did never see or hear the rolling calf myself, but people say he was the duppie of a bloodthirsty murder-er, so wicked that not even a good funeral with all the proper sweeping and sprinkling and thing could hold him in the ground. I was determine to hear this rolling calf for myself and use to lay wake at night, my head under the covers, but months pass and I never even as much as hear cow-hoof, so I put it away back of my mind.

One night it was raining, real soft-like on the zinc, pat, and it stop, then pat, and it stop again, then pat, and on like that. It was the kinda rain that sound as if it waiting for an answer, almost like a knocking. The rain bring all kinda story and thing, you know. That's why I like listen to it. I use to sleep on a cot in the front room, and outside I could see a little piece of moon hanging up in the blue-black looking like someone broken thumbnail. Every now and then a drop of rain hit gainst the window, and sparkle, pat, so soon the window-glass was scat-ter all over with the shine rain drops them, just like a piece of star-sky come down. Glory. The bed was well sweet that night, and I let my head sink way down inna the pillow, and I close my eyes and listen to the rain calling my name, I-da. I-da. Just like that, over and over, the sound taking me away, joy unspeakable. And then I hear like some-thing pulling on the ground, real soft-like and real slow. Dragging drag-ging dragging through the dry-up leaves in the mango walk. Lord-a-mighty, when the drum in my chest realize what going on, it start batta out a tune, Ba-duup, Ba-duup, like I did never hear it carry on with before. Ba-duup, Ba-duup. Ba-duup, Ba-duup. I put my head under the pillow and cover myself from head to toe because I was sure the rolling calf would hear the drum and come find me. Ba-duup, Ba-duup. Ba-duup, Ba-duup. The drum start to pick up speed, Ba-baBa-ba-duup, Ba-

baBa-ba-duup, and Lord, I was flat on my back with nothing to do but wait and listen. Then when it seem like the night did stretch itself out pass where it should already end, it come clear that the rolling calf was walking around in circles but he wasn't coming any nearer to the yard, and I start to realize something: The sound this chain making, dragging through the mango walk, did have a kinda sadness to it—a loneliness, you know what I mean? And after I calm down and listen good, is as if something grab at my heart-ears and a feeling overtake me in the bed, and I *knew* this calf was not a wicked calf at all, not at all.

So, what to do? Next morning, I tell my mother everything. Mama was frying fritters on the coal stove, and she listen to me all quiet-quiet without even as much as saying a word. When I finish, Mama still don't say nothing. She put the fritters in a plate. She cover the plate with a pot cover. She wrap the plate and the pot cover with a dish cloth. She tie the dish cloth in a knot. And stare at it. Then, she turn and look at me all stern-like (but I could tell there was fright standing up in her two eye them), and she say, "Ida, don't lemme hear one more word from you bout any duppie foolishness. People around here already mark you as a bad luck, someting-gone-wrong chile. Don't let dem goat mouth catch up with you." Mama turn her back to me. She put on some water to boil. She start grating a little cocoa. And I knew that was the end of that.

Anyway, next night I was right back there on the cot ready to listen out again, but not a sound. Third night, same thing. Fourth night, still the same thing—not even as much as a mongoose dragging fowl feathers through the yard. On the fifth night it start to rain, this time the drops knocking up gainst one another and howling, Lord, what a howling all the way till daylight. Sixth night, more wailing and howling, all hell let loose on the red clay yard. Seventh night I lay there listen to the batta-batta and the knock-knock on the little piece o' zinc roof, trying to make sense of the drops them, till gradual things settle down to just a whimper and a mild spit-spit gainst the window glass. The clouds start to move from across the moon, just like someone parting a piece o' gauze curtain, slow and sneakified, to peep out at things. I watch, and as I watch the moon become more and more brazen and bareface so that soon the clouds them all drawn apart and resting to one side. Shh.

The breadfruit leaves stop swaying. There was a hush. A kinda wait-ing. Me and the house and the moon and the trees inna the yard and all the little grass-quit line up on the branches—just waiting. In the moon-shine I could see a little lizard on the windowsill, her pointy head raise up and tilt to one side, and she listen along with the rest of we. They say moonshine is poor woman jewels, you know. And is true. That night I woulda never give it up for all the treasure in the world. Light glistening on the wet leaves and grass—just like diamonds, just like silver, just like crystal. And the little moonshine lizard! Glass beads line up all along her backbone, a true-true queen.

When the dragging come it was soft and timid-like, coming up all slow through the bush, then stopping. Coming, then stopping again. I hold my breath, and the corner of my mind which keep the deep-and-wide eyes see the calf stopping to look out through the mango leaf at the asleep house, then moving on again, and all the time he hold his head to the ground like this, you know, sniffing for the barefoot, wide toe tracks of the living. The drum was beating steady in my chest and I slip on my dress and tiptoe to the front door. But stick a pin, sister-chile—

Here comes Nurse Watson and I have to pretend to take my medicine. All these little yellow pills. Pro zag-zig zac and what-not, what-have-you. When she leave the room, I'll just slip it from under my tongue and pick up with you again. In the meantime, put the calabash to your ear and listen. In the beginning it won't sound like anything special, and then it will sound like tongues, but keep listening long enough and your heart-ears will begin to understand. Go on. Whether you do or you don't, they'll still think you mad, so you might as well go ahead and try. Don't pay the medicine tray any mind; we don't really need it—is just their trick to keep us fool. Close your eyes. Breathe, long-ears woman, breathe. That's right; whoosh, whoosh, hear it?

Two

COME, TAKE A BREAK. Let's walk out in the yard, away from this urine stench. That old woman over there, Mrs. Johnskin, always wetting herself, the poor thing, and they wouldn't even change her sheets. One ole woman knows another, and trust me, she don't belong in here any more than you or me or the ole Queen of What-not. You know, this Nurse Watson walk with her toes pointed out, one foot going left, the other going right, just like a woman we had in our district years ago. What was her name again? . . . I just had it at the tip of my tongue . . .

Come anyway, at least outside here in the yard we can feel a little breeze on our face and admire the periwinkle. These little flowers just about the only bright thing around this place, you know. Every now and then, when I stand middle-day with the sun right over my head, it seem to me like one of them wink at me, real quick, as if they don't want anyone else to notice. Because of this I call them my 'winkles. People don't like to let anybody know they glimpse little things like that, you know, that's why they rub their eye and walk away and miss the rest of it.

. . . Can't remember her name for the life of me . . . She used to have a hook nose like a parrot . . . and she was a deaconess in the church . . . and she did have a pair of eye's glasses. Ahh, Miles, that's it, Sister Miles. Sister Miles did have a kind of half-laugh with a crack in it, and

when I was a child she have a way of laughing the laugh and patting her
lap for me to come sit with her. Then she fix her eye's glass on her nose
(she was the only one in the district who have eye's glasses and she did
well proud of it) and search my face, righteous you know like this, then
she ask me if I know, hallelujah, that there's ten, blessed-be-the-Lord
commandments, not seven, not eight, praise him, not even nine, hal-
leloo, but ten, oh yes, and all the while she squeezing my fingers
between her two tablet of stone. Afterward, she take a paradise plum
from outta her purse and put it in my hand-middle and smile at me all
nice, but I could smell a foulness coming from outta the pit in her
throat and I never trust her, so every time I see her I start catch fraid
that more of my fingers or even my toes them would start fall off. And
I begin to wonder, why always so much hair in my comb? Is it because
I steal two of Marse Thomas bombay mango? And why my finger nails
always tearing and breaking so? Is it because I spit in Teacher Brown
tea when she wasn't looking? The hog, she deserved it, she rough me
up in front the whole class for reciting that poem (the one with all the
nice behaving flowers) by that Wordswool or Woolwords (I can't
remember which) wrong. Tribulation. This worrying went on and on,
till when I grow little more big and my teeth begin fall, I fret so till I
decide to tell Mama. Mama listen all quiet and say not to mind Sister
Miles for Sister Miles is a busy-body. It wasn't till years later, when I
reach third-book, that I come to understand that Sister Miles and the
other bad-minded brethren wasn't talking bout my sin them at all, but
Mama own, for it was believe, you know, that Mama must be partake
of, or watch, or listen to some evil someting herself in order to end up
with a nine-finger baby.

Anyway, I say all this to say that by the time I was around twelve and
listening out for the rolling calf, I make up my mind that I wasn't going
married and I wasn't going have children—no, Ma'm, no way—because
I, Ida, did not want them born with any missing limbs. As much badness
as I use to carry on with, I was sure-sure they would be lame and bed-
strick. But this thing had a turn side you know, for it leave me free to carry
on with as much badness as I like without worrying about what going hap-

pen to my pickney them. So there I was tiptoeing through the front door on my way to meet the rolling calf.

Now use the deep-and-wide eye that keep inna the corner of your mind and picture this: me, stealing out cross the guinea grass in my ragga-ragga dress (I was a mawga thing then, no bigger than a mus-mus), the moonshine following me, lighting up my bare foot-bottom them, quick light like this, flash flash flash, every time I lift up one foot and put the other one down. Everything quiet. Everything still. Just the sound of my bare foot on the wet grass. Shomp. Shomp. Now hush up and try to listen me, a dragging, dragging, dragging something, all soft-like, all slow.

That night, the closer I come to the mango walk, the more my heart-ears let me know that this calf was not a calf that come to bother me. This calf was not a wicked calf. This calf was not after blood. By the time I get to the edge of the trees, I hear the dragging clear-clear, and I hear another sound—the cow foot stepping in and out of the wet leaf them. Something switch on inside o' me then, and it come to me that there was a kind of fraidiness in the way the calf walking. Same time as this come to me, I see like a shadow or something cross through the trees. The drum in my chest start to carry on, and I stand still and I watch and I listen, the moon waiting right there with me. At first I couldn't see nothing, only tree bark and branch, but after my eyes set-tle, I make out the little calf between two stringy mango tree, such a young thing with him chain around him neck. I edge a little closer and I see the eyes, all big and frighten in the moonshine, the skin on him neck trembling. I step closer again, but the calf step back from me, his chain dragging and making a little noise on the ground. So we stand there, the two of us eyes making four, quiet and still, watching one another, wondering what going to happen next.

There we was for I don't know how long—time did on a different track. Then perhaps because it come clear that I didn't mean no harm, or perhaps because I was, after all, just a knotty-hair young girl in a ragga-ragga dress with bare foot, to this day I still not sure why, but the calf step forward, about a distance of two yards from me, sniffing out a circle round my feet, his chain marking out a trail that circle me in the dirt and the leaf. Two time the calf walk around me, and two time I hold my breath; my foot root in the ground and I couldn't move it. My body stiff, like my neck have gum in it, so that even though the calf sniffing his way around me, I couldn't even turn my head to watch him. Each time I wait for him to come from behind me, and each time he come around, still sniffing, watching the ground, you know, his little ears all prick up just like this. By now, the drum in my chest beating out all kinda beat, and then, on the third time a funny thing happen: I make out the sound of another drum, answering mine, Ba-duup, Ba-duup. Beat for beat, drum for drum. Ba-duup, Ba-duup, coming from outta the calf. Ba-duup, Ba-duup, I take in a deep breath and wait for him to make his circle, but this time, what come walking from behind me was not the little calf at all.

People say that if trees could talk, they would have so many story to tell that everyone ears would grow way down to their shoulders. Well, let me tell you: Trees talk, we just don't listen. Where you think this calabash come from? A tree, of course. (But we'll get to that in a minute.)

That night as I stand in the moonshine circle at the edge of the mango grove, what come walking from behind me was not a little calf at all. Not at all. I could hear his step with the same fraidiness, and the same sadness, so soft and careful. And I still hear his chain, dragging, dragging on the ground. His drum keep up the batta-batta with mine, beat for beat. Ba-duup, Ba-duup. But what come and stand before me was not the little calf, uh-uh, not the little brown calf. Not the little brown calf with the teeny-tiny horns. What come and stand before me was a young boy, about fourteen or so, naked from the waist on up, an iron collar round his neck, and a chain that dangle all the way to the ground.

The periwinkle have a story they like to ponder. It is the story of a girl who was put up for sale on the auction block down by the bay. This was many, many years ago, when guns at the fort were still used to fire salutes to admirals and lords on holidays and anniversaries, or sometimes it seemed, for no reason at all. The guns sent a shiver through the stems of the periwinkles, the soft soil shifting around their roots, ants losing their grip.

The periwinkle say, the girl on the auction block was young and brown. She had been washed down and oiled so that her skin shone in the sunlight; an iron chain was attached to her leg and hooked to a post nearby. When the auctioneer stepped forward, his voice, boomed, ONE STRONG MANDINGO WENCH, ONE-EYED, BUT SOUND AS A POUND, and the crowd pressed closer, but the periwinkle remember that the girl appeared distracted, seeming not even to notice the growing throng, much less hear the voice of the auctioneer. With her one good eye, she was looking way past them—past the tops of their plumed hats, past the hill and the fort of a hundred guns, her eye was focused someplace beyond the sugarcane fields and dirt roads, and even past where the land again met the sea on the other side of the island. A man with a wooden cane stepped forward. He examined her teeth, looked into her eyes, but still the girl looked right through him. He tapped her lightly with his cane on each shoulder, on each buttock, on each leg; then smiling, he held her breasts in the palms of his hands. GOING AT EIGHT, GOING . . .

This is what the periwinkle remember: the girl, suddenly bursting into uncontrollable laughter, her head flung back, one arm raised, a long dark finger pointing at something in the distance which only she could see. They all followed her finger—the auctioneer, the man with the cane, and all the plumed hats—turning in unison, peering across their shoulders, trying to make out the object of her delight. But because the heart-eye sees differently, and because their own hearts were without eye, they saw nothing . . .

Mad wench! Their heads spun forward now, annoyed. This is what the auctioneer saw, what the man with the cane saw, what the plumed hats saw: the platform empty; the wench gone. Disappeared—her chain still hooked to its post.

Look. Look. Look. This is what the periwinkle see: a small brown lizard crawling leisurely across the stones, and away from the crowd.

Three

I TELL YOU THIS STORY because I think you need to hear it, and because I want you to know that there is more to this world than what you think you see floating on top the pot. See that sea out there cross the bay? That sea have many stories to tell. There are things bury at the bottom of that sea that woulda make you break out in cold sweat if you ever find it all out.

Speaking of which, the other day me and Mrs. Johnskin sit in the ward just laughing at ourselves. Talking bout how neither of us ever did learn how to swim, or drive car, or even ride bicycle. Mrs. Johnskin say she spend three months over in foreign, and the white people she work for just couldn't believe she live in Jamaica all her life and never swim in the Caribbean. Lord help us, but you know what? And this is the part I want you to understand: Some of us ole people don't know swims, but plenty of us can walk on water.

Listen good. I wasn't always an ole woman. I use to be a mawga girl, with a ragga-ragga dress and bare foot. But is a funny thing, ever since that night in the moonshine when I see that boy with the iron collar around him neck, I been feeling like an ole ole woman. I looked at that collar, and is as if from the moment I set my eyes on it, I start to pick up years. To this day, I hate to have anything dangling around my neck. Because of that, even if you give me a dainty little gold chain string with this and that queen's jewels, I just couldn't wear it. I just can't stand the feel of it.

Anyway, there I was standing before this young man with his chain dangling from him neck. He was a bit taller than me, his face all dirty and scratch-up; his eyes big and sad, just like the little calf own. He did look tired, as if he did traveling from a long way, and I could tell he need food and water and a place to sleep, but my tongue was gum to my mouth-top, and I just couldn't speak. All this time, his drum still beat with strength, answering mine. Ba-duup, Ba-duup, back and forth. He stretch his arms, Ba-ba duup duup, and put something round and smooth in my two hands—ba-duup. Heh, I was frighten, I tell you, because all this time I didn't know he did carry as much as a nutmeg. I hold the thing up to the moonlight, and see that it was a calabash. My arms them feel weak, and I almost drop it, even as light as it was. His eyes smile a bit then, and he just turn and walk away in the trees. I did want to say something, but I just stand there, a mawga ole woman with a ragga-ragga dress and bare foot.

But come with me, step this way. Here come that volunteer lady and is time for us to go inside for crafts. She don't come by often, maybe once a week or so, but when she come, she give bits of this and that to make whatever we want. A nice lady, I think. Sometimes she act sort of fraidy-fraidy, but I think she have a good heart. Last month, I ask her to bring us some straw and I teach some of the women here how to make baskets. My Mama and Papa was good with straw, you know, and don't let anybody tell you that basket weaving is only fool-fool people work because is not true. Most of who you see out there criticizing, well, ask them to weave you a basket and see if they would know how. Oh, I so glad she here today! She promise to bring me some clay and I think I going to mold a little lizard to decorate the floor beside my bed. If you going to be lock up in a place like this, you might as well do whatever it take to keep you busy. There's a little brown polly lizard that I keep see wiggling around outside in the yard, and I think I going make one just like that. If it was left to Nurse Watson, we wouldn't do any crafts here at all, you know. She see us sitting here happy, making our little this and making our little that, and she seem to think we up to tricks instead of crafts. I can't wait to see the expression on her big pumpkin face when she see my lizard.

I never did see the rolling calf after that night. Perhaps he accomplish whatever he did come for and gone at last, to rest. But with my heart-ears, I still hear him: the chain, dragging dragging, the heart, beating, beating . . .

Four

LISTEN. PITTER-PAT, PAT-PAT. Is raining again, and your ears already growing longer, I can tell. I can tell. Perhaps I should ask the volunteer lady to bring us few gourds for crafts next month! We could all make little pots and bowls and cut out nice marks around the sides. Pitter-pat, pat-pat.

This is what I like about polly lizards: If you cut off their tails, they grow another one right back. Now that's what you call a back-answer polly.

Five

THIS CALABASH YOU SEE here—half in my basket, half in my brassiere—well, is the same-same one that the young boy did give me in the moonshine so many years ago. That night, I take it home, wrap it up in an ole dish cloth, and hide it under my bed because the last thing I did want was for Mama or Papa to find it and catch fraid. Every morning after that I bend down and peep on it, just to make sure it still there. When it dry, I make like I was going to river to catch water, and I hide it in my water pan and I take off. Down river, I find a nice warm rock in the sun, and I sit and cut the calabash in half and scoop out the inside, and as you see, I been carrying the two half around with me to this day.

Now that day on the warm rock, I sit there and I consider, and I consider. I did know that duppie like shade under calabash tree, and I did know that my navel string (misbury, mind you) under one of them, but what the iron-collar-boy mean by delivering this trouble-fruit right into my two hand? One mind tell me to dash the calabash inna the river and be done with it, but another one tell me to keep it and wait, and that's what I did. I wait. I turn the calabash this way. I turn it that way. I shine it up with a little coconut oil, and at night I keep it on my pillow beside me. I take my Mama pen-knife and I carve up the sides with leaves and flowers and a little lizard with the head turn to the side, all attention, just like the one on the windowsill the moonshine night. Still, I didn't know what else to do with it, so I start put the calabash to my ear, and I listen good, and I hear a sound something like what you hear in seashells: Whoosh. Whoosh. And that's how I would fall sleep at night. Whoosh. Whoosh. I begin to dream dreams bout rain falling falling and drum beating beating; and all the time twelve hand beating twelve drum and twelve foot keeping up time, and such a tum-tum and such a carrying on, but I never could see the owner of the hand them and I never could see the owner of the foot. Later, I would wake up, my owna drum battering out all loud inside me.

Nothing worse than a secret gathering up size, ready to bust out inna you. I did want tell Mama bout the calabash so bad, but I know she woulda scold me, and I know she woulda fraid for me, and for herself, and she woulda never really listen. One morning I wake and find her standing over me, one half of the calabash waving in her hand. "What this?" she say and you shoulda see the wrath of hell stand up like two fist in her nose hole them, widening them out, but I never answer her. I was fraid, and I did feel ole. He hear her voice and Papa come to the door, wondering what happen. Mama throw the calabash cross the room, and she just barely miss the puss on the floor. Papa bend and grope around, and he pick up the calabash from where it rock in the corner. I brace myself, and Mama fling up her arm. "Play with puppie, puppie lick yu mout!" and her voice rise up like hurricane Matty when it did wheel and tun and wheel and tun and blow off the roof.

Later that night I lie down in bed and I hear Mama and Papa talking. "This chile is a strange one for true, Selma."

You know, if you don't have anybody to listen to you, your tongue can wither and dry just like rotten tamarind. So that's why I start tell myself to myself, and I start sing and whisper inna the dark like an ole ole woman, and this is what I find out: the trees in the yard, them listen me, and the flowers in Mama garden, them listen me, and the duppie them in the calabash, them listen me. Even Madam Fate that grow in her secret place, she listen me.

Six

I DID MEET BELLA when I was fifteen. She talk to me from out the calabash. Just a teeny-tiny little voice, calling, "Ida! Ida!" By this time I was
hiding the calabash in a hole dig downa river. I did stop going to school
and I was taking in washing and ironing to help out little bit. I use to
spread the clothes out on the rock them by the riverside, and while I
wait for them to dry, I use to like put the calabash to my ears and
breathe, and hear the whoosh whoosh whoosh and just lie down inna
the soft grass.

Bella's voice catch me by surprise—soft you know, but like something gone wrong. I didn't know where to turn. You say, maybe is magine I magine it? No, the voice did clear. Someone call my name, Ida. I
hear it plain-plain. Plain as you hear my owna voice talk to you right
now inna this Garden. For two days after that, there wasn't a sound
more. And then she come again, this time bawling, bawling, bawling,
one piece o' bawling. Mercy. Don't ever make the mistake of believing
that all the dead them rest in peace, you know. Some of them can rest,
yes, but some of them more restless than you and me. Unfinish business, that's what it is. Then there is some long-dead who turn busy-
body because they trying to catch your eye; they want you to remember them.

Bella did restless because she did still need to have her say and set a few things straight. She was twelve, you know, when one night, the overseer-man rape her and drown her in the sea. Her body did never find, and no one did ever know the truth of why she disappear. This was way back, before your time and mine, and the people in the Great House send out three big barking dog to sniff her out. The dogs them track her to the beach, but no one did ever understand why all of a sudden, all three of them stop at the water side and stare out on the sea, hollering.

Bella tell me how to find the place where her body ravish. The poor soul, she did need a witness, and the lot fall on me. How I coulda refuse? Believe me, the dead not to be taken light. Later I search for the spot, and find it—a small little place grown up with sea-grape. I did see a fisherman there that morning. I watch him haul in his boat, his net empty. It did windy, and after the fisherman leave, I just stand there on the beach with my ragga-ragga dress blowing around my legs and my calabash to my ears. I listen and I listen till something like a prickle-breeze rise up inna me, and I hear the sound of foot running. Bare foot. A young girl bare foot. I hear the overseer boot them. I hear a scuffle. A scream. A scuffle. A small winjie voice like something hold over the mouth. Heavy breath. A small winjie voice. Heavy breath. A small winjie voice. The sea swoosh swoosh. The sea swoosh swoosh. Mercy.

I meet other friends from inna the calabash as well, you know. There's a family of five whose grave did root up when the government bulldoze their land for some fool project or another. I write letter to the minister of this and the minister of that tracing them out nicely, but you know how these high-up people don't listen nobody. Anyway, I scratch the family names on that rock over there. That way they can get respect and memberance, at least by me. Is the best I can do. See, there's the little boy, name Evan, and the two girl them, Millicent and Shirley, and the father, Horace, and the mother, Doreen. Doreen was the last one to pass, you know, she dead from worry and hungry belly. The only thing leave to her name was a five-dollar tie up in a hanky, so the neighbor them did all pitch in to dig her a grave out inna the yard with her husband and children. Well, that all bulldoze and gone now, but at least they have this rock inna the Garden . . .

But back to Bella. For years afterward, I never hear another word from her, and I think to myself: Bella must be resting in peace. Then one day, I sitting on a rock by my usual river spot, and a voice call, Ida! Ida! I knew her voice right away, but this time it did fill with power and this is the part that did frighten me: She say she was back in the *flesh*. There is something about an angry duppie that don't ever give up. This Bella still had unfinish business, and as it turns out, she was back for her second chance. Every now and then it happens: A woman, dead for years and years, gather up her strength and drag herself up out of the sea, wet and naked as the day she born, her hair bushy-bushy with seaweed. They say that all of them come up laughing; they hold their head high and walk straight out of the water and not a soul guess their secret. That's just what that kin-owl, Bella, did. She came back and not a soul knew who she was. Years pass now and still me and Bella talk through the calabash like good-good friends—she tell me all her spirit-sorrow—but not even I know who she really is. Sometimes I wonder if she coulda be Johnskin or that volunteer lady or one of the washer woman them. I wonder what kinda flesh-sorrow she have?

Then there's some dead that don't need comfort, but they provide comfort. Take Madda Wilma, for instance. She tell me she know how to make rain fall and things, and she take me up under her wing and teach me. I not the best, you know, but I can rustle up a storm when I need it. My calabash double like a rainpan: I have a few handful of rice that I drop in it; the rice go pitter-pat, pat-pat, like that, and that's how I find a voice for calling. Pitter-pat, pat-pat. In this rain-business, you has to be patient. You has to watch and listen. You has to be willing to take a chance. But, ahh, in the distance you see it—a small dark cloud.

Madda Wilma and them travel through the calabash from far-far to comfort me, they tell story bout all kinda crisscrossing and falling down, and rising up and tuning round. But what I listen out for the most is the voice of my own children—April, May, and June (name

after the month they born in). Night time, I hear them call out to me,
"Mama," and the drum in my chest jump up, bam! Ahh, you did think
I never did have children, eh? Heh, come let me bruck story give you.

Seven

I NEVER DID WANT TO marry Rupert. His teeth was always mossy and he did have a club foot, which wasn't his fault, I know, but when you really don't want be with somebody every little this and every little that come like a big nuisance. Beside all that, I did confide in him bout the iron-collar-boy, and he laugh (Rupert had a way to laugh and talk louder than everybody else) and call it a heap o' hog wash. I marry Rupert to please Mama and Papa and because there weren't any other way out. Mama say, "Everyone think you is a someting-gone-wrong girl, you shoulda be glad a nice man like Rupert looking at you." I was twenty-what-not and still taking in washing and ironing. I did have the calabash and five shillings to my name. I did have knotty hair, bare foot, and one ragga-ragga dress. Rupert come to me like a road outta the bush.

For each of three years them I spend with Rupert I receive three daughters—April, May, and June—all o' them still-born. God bless their little souls, they see the condition of the house I was living in, the condition of the island, the condition of the world, and they decide to save their breath. How I can blame them? Rupert and me live in a little board-up house in town. We live in a yard with a half-dozen or so little room just like our own, there was always plenty-plenty music, plenty baby crying, plenty kas-kas and jing-bang pot-throwing and praying

and singing and all kinda moaning and carryings-on. Mercy. I did do
domestic work for a family up in the hills, and Rupert did do a little yard
work here and there whenever he coulda find it. I never did grow to love
Rupert but I grow to bear him. I bear his mossy teeth and him club
foot, and I bear up his body on top o' mine. Night time when I sure he
sleeping, I pull the calabash from outta the hiding place under the bed,
and put it to my ears, straining to listen. It was during this time that I
meet a little girl, Vashti, who did die from dengue fever on the very spot
the yard was build. She sing for me sweet-sweet and in a high-high
voice and in a language I never understand. When my daughters still-
born she take them in her care, and I know they was safe.

One thing I can say about Rupert is that he did have ambition. He
did always talk bout becoming his own man. By this time, that big
world war was over and there was notice stick up everywhere in town,
advertising for people to go to England and work. Tribulation. Rupert
did have a feeling he could make it big in England, so he take his time
and save a penny here, save a penny there (he was always good with
money), and next thing you know he did have his fare for the *Andrea
Gritti*. I remember the day he leave; it was the year of my third baby,
and it was an October and a Thursday. I remember it well because I did
have to ask Mrs. DeSouza for the day off so I coulda see him leave at
the docks. Lord, you shoulda see the amount of people waiting to get
the boat! If the sea could talk, I tell you, it woulda have some story to
tell. Rupert leave with his teeth mossy as ever and grinning like a wild
ass. The plan was that he woulda send for me after three months, but
sister-chile, I wait and I wait till I almost blue, and to this day, after people all gone to the moon and come back, I still don't even hear as much
as a squeak from Rupert. Miss Eunice' nephew, Robert, (the one that
works at the airport) say that his auntie was over in England and see
Rupert working in Someting-burg at a kind of factory place. But I don't
want to go on too much about Rupert. Let bygones be bygones, I have
business to take care of. There's that nice lady who work in the
kitchen. Every now and then, she sneak me a little treat. A piece of
cheese, or a little jam for that dry bread they give us. Come. Hurry.

Cho, she's on her way out. I suppose there's no treats today. If it weren't for the kindness of a few good people, I don't now how I woulda make it in this place. Is the kindness of my calabash friend them which did keep me going after Rupert leave. Now I want you to understand, is not that I was pining after Rupert, no way, not me. But Rupert leave me in hot molasses. I couldn't live and pay the rent on just my little money alone, so what else I coulda do but go home? And that's what I did. I take the bus straight back to the bush, home to Mama and Papa.

Eight

LORD HAVE MERCY, every time they don't know what to do with we, they put we in the Garden. Last night they bring another woman here. See her sit down over there on the bed by the wall, the youngish one in the yellow dress. All night she stay up singing a little song, *hickory dickory dock*, now what that could mean? I don't know yet, but let me wait and see.

Anyway, while Nurse Watson have her back turn, there's someting else I want to show you. Look in my pocket. Inside of it full up with scrapses—little bits of this and that—a button from my mother funeral dress, a string from here, a bit of hair from there and a heap o' periwinkle. Night time, I keep my things hide under the mattress where no one will find them. Is funny how these periwinkle look mischievous, like if you give them a half-chance, they woulda even take root and grow up from outta my pocket just to back-answer me for picking them.

But there's one thing that bruck me up: I don't hear a word from Mama and Papa since they dead. You woulda think they would speak to me from out the calabash like everyone else, but no, they holding back. Hard-head even in death. They both dead with ole people trouble, you know—pressure and sugar. Papa did go first, the poor soul, and Mama soon after. I stay with them right up till the end. Before she dead, Mama whisper to me in her hoarse voice, "Leave that trouble-fruit alone, Ida. Leave it, and go seek the Lord." Oh, Mama . . .

After that, I live in the old house by myself, still taking in washing and ironing and doing this and that odd job. Rupert, did gone for a good ten years by this time, but I can't say I did miss the bastard at all. I did glad for the fresh air and peace in country where I coulda relax and listen. Twice a week I go into town to sell a few orange, a head or two of yam, a few breadfruit and so on. But other than that, I keep to myself, I listen my calabash, and when I not listening, I carve some up to sell in the market. People think I did strange—a unmarry woman living up in that ole house all by herself and with all them funny-looking gourd stand up on the verandah. I coulda feel it from the way they look at me from out their corner-eye. Is not that I did never want company, but I did already mark as gone-wrong from way way back, and people use to think I coulda goozoo them, so them stay away from me. So that's how the voice them in the calabash come to friend me up. I know all about them, and them know all about me. The house did full.

It so full, that it take a long time after Mama dead before I realize that I did stop talk to anyone at all other than a word or two: "Yes, Ma'm." "Thank you, Ma'm." People see me pass with my basket on my head, and most of them drop their eye, but some of them nod and I just nod back. Perhaps in some strange kinda way, they did understand or they did overstand, I not sure which. So this is how the voice them in the calabash get turn up even more loud.

Over the years hard work shrivel up the body. I did struggling to make two ends meet, and I plant more but selling less, and all the time I get more ole and more tired. Sometimes when the sun hot, I use to go town and stop and rest by the door of that big Citizen's bank so I coulda feel the cool of the air condition every time the glass doors them open and close. One time a customer complain, say every time she go bank, she see me stand up and stare and pick my nose by the door, so anyway, a manager come out and ask me to leave. I look at him, my eyes them steady as a nanny goat, and I just pick up my basket and walk off. From then I start sit in front the hotel them near the sea, but the unmannersable tourist them couldn't stop watch me from behind their sun's glasses, and some of them even stop and snap me, brazen. When they carry on like that, I just give them my look and they turn away quick time.

I was going town more often now, I sell my few little things, and evening I take the bus back home. By this time, I did always so tired, and I couldn't remember a time when I not tired—all them years carrying water bucket on my head, and doing Mrs. So-and-So laundry or climbing up this hill and down that gully, and chopping sugarcane like any man. After living from shackle to shackle, I did just want sit down for a change and listen myself breathe.

One of my best spot where nobody hassle me was by the side of the house where I coulda sit under the poinciana tree that spread like one of those wide-rimmed straw hat Mama and Papa use to make. In the early days I did save my daughter navel string and bury them under this tree (where my own string shoulda bury in the first place). The tree all flourish now, you should see it. Everybody pass the tree say how the tree pretty and how it strive, and I feel so proud. At night my daughters whisper me from out the calabash, I hear their voice calling, "Mama," and I see their arms them thin as bamboo sticks reach for me, but when I try to touch them nothing in my hand excepting the dark.

Anyway, is one day in town while I resting and catching my breath on the court house steps that I did have a vision. I see God. God was a woman with a skin like cinnamon, and when she smile her eye-corners them fold just like three neat starch pleats on the side of her face. Her teeth them straight and even, and I did so happy when I don't see any gaps between them because I know full and well that a woman with too much gaps in her mouth would just quickly swallow up my words without really hearing what it is I have to say. She dress up nice in a purple dashiki with yellow trimming around the sleeves and hem, but she was barefoot, and from the mud and the callous skin, I could tell she come from far-far. She touch my face, and her hands them cool-cool like the glass doors on the Citizen's bank. No one did touch me in years. She never say not a thing, but she call my name, "Ida," and she say it so clear and nice that, believe me, is as if each letter call out like a bell. By this time I did spend so much time living alone up in that ole bruck-down house that I did even forget that anyone at all, much less God, even know my name. She never stay long but when she leave I see a tangerine in my basket, and I know it was God bless, just for me. Look, after all this time the tangerine all shrivel, but I still have few seeds—here, yes you—smell them.

After that, I go to the court house time and time again, hoping, you know, that I woulda catch a glimpse of her. I roam the streets, walking up and down, looking for the purple dashiki, but never see it. Sometimes in my mind, I call her name, "God!" but she never answer. Then the thought come to me, perhaps I calling her by the wrong name, so I try Lord, Jehovah, Jah . . . but none of them seem to fit her, and she keep quiet, so inna my heart I make up my owna name for her, Shiki, like *dashiki*.

Is following this that for the first time in years I raise my voice and scream right out loud: "Shiki! Shiki!" and I did so frighten by the sound of my own tongue inna my own mouth, resurrect just like Lazarus and so clear. I remember the last time I did ever speak out like that. It was at Mama funeral. I did wear a black dress with white buttons down the front, the same dress I wear to Papa funeral. I remember how I look at her in the casket and touch her face. It did feel like the leather on new church shoes, and never look like her at all. Her hair did part on the wrong side and her hands them the color of some beige curtains we use to hang at the window. When I go down on the floor and bawl out her name, "Mama!" they did have to carry me outside. "Mama" was the last word I ever speak with that kinda striving. Is as if when I try call her from the dead, all the neck-string in my throat stand up so tight, they strain and pop and something leave from outta me and drain me of all strength.

Ha. Now I did find myself opening my mouth and shouting out to Shiki on street corner, looking through store window and stepping inside and studying the face them. One time I did sure I see her. I notice a piece o' purple something moving through the crowd in the market, and I run after it and call her. I jump over yam and sweet potato and cassava and all kinda thing, and I nearly knock over a woman, her hands full with water coconut—but it was only a rasta man with a purple t-shirt. He was nice, though. "Peace and love, sister," that's what he say.

I begin to talk with Shiki. I tell her bout the Bible I have at home which did belong to my grandmother, and bout my owna mother, Selma, who use to read me it from the big Home-Sweet-Home kerosene lamp. I tell her bout April, May, and June and bout Rupert—who, by now, rumor did have it, collapse and dead one afternoon in a barber shop in London. I tell her bout how I tired and how sometime all I have strength for is just to breathe—pulling air and pushing it out, pulling air and pushing it out one breath at a time. Whenever I did use to see girls with thin fingers just like my daughter April own woulda been, it make me feel drain as if all strength just trickle out my eyes. And the color yellow (I know it woulda been May's favorite color)— it make my joints feel weak as if parts of me might start fall off. Yellow did everywhere: in the market, on the store front them, the cassia flowers. And as for a high squeaky-squeaky voice like June's—I just couldn't stand it. I tell God how in time like this I reach quick-quick for my calabash, and listen for the whoosh whoosh, and how I turn it up high or low, however it please me. I couldn't see Shiki, but I did know she watch and listen, and I know she understand. A few time, I hear her laugh, such a true-true laugh, like the kind of laugh you laugh when you sitting around roasting corn and cashew and telling 'Nancy story. I was please I coulda make God laugh.

(Now I want you to relax and listen this part good. Nurse Watson gone to gossip with the other nurse them over in Ward Three, so don't worry, she not going be back for a while . . .)

I did on my way home one evening when I see Shiki again. There she was over by the banana tree them on the Howard property. She did have her back turn away from me and walking through the trees like she going down by the river. I try call out her name, "Shiki!" but I so excited that the word couldn't come out, it stop up in my throat like a big ole guinep seed that can't climb past my tongue. I begin to run toward her. But how fast can an ole woman run? I keep my eyes fix on the purple dashiki moving in and out of the banana tree them, but is as if every time I think I get close to God, she all of a sudden look farther away. The drum in my chest did going Ba-duup, Ba-duup; I have one hand holding my hat down on my head, like this, the other holding on to my basket. Ba-duup, Ba-duup. By the time I get to the river, she disappear. I call out "Shiki!" and this time the word came out full-full and clear, but it did too late. I was tired. So tired. But happy that I did at least glimpse her.

This is what I remember: laying down on the grass to catch my breath; looking up into the sky. It spread for yards and yards like a big orange and yellow tie-dye. The breeze did soft, I remember it well—so comforting, just like the breath of a child. A smile spread cross my face like a please-puss and I keep my eyes fix on one small dark cloud shape like a calabash. I hear a whoosh whoosh whoosh, soft and far like someone humming a hymn. I just lay there pulling air and pushing out, pulling air and pushing out, pulling air . . . then pushing . . . I did relax my grip on the basket, the shrivel tangerine roll cross the grass and settle.

Nine

SOMETHING ABOUT TRYING to remember how things did happen help me understand *why* them happen. You can never listen too much you know, that's why I glad your ears growing longer. Come, put the calabash to your ears and close your eyes.

The white coats did find me on the river bank, my eyes them fix, watching the sky. But what they coulda know bout calabash anyway? They strap me up inside a van, and all the while I whisper, "Shiki!"

Night time, and it's raining in the Garden. Lightly. Softly. Each drop lingering. Gliding down, gently down. This rain could be a slow dance. This rain could be a symphony. This rain could be a poem. A soul-chant. A love letter. A sister-song.

The periwinkle are quiet, their pierced centers wet and glistening. Shhh.

The little brown lizard hops to the entrance of Ward One, her inquisitive head tilted to the side.

Such rain could only have been called through much heart-knowing.

Gracie

A lone woman sits on a rock and looks out to sea. She looks and sighs. Looks and sighs, and remembers her daughters who were sold away to a man in a black top hat, visiting the island from Louisiana. After all these years she can still hear their voices, high-pitched and broken, "Mama! Mama!" Now the woman thinks to herself: What good is freedom when the sea is still wide and the horizon curves shut like the steel bolt of a padlock?

One

EVERY DAY ON MY WAY to school and on my way home, I pass Periwinkle Garden. The security guard, ole Mr. Cameron, usually half-sleep, so I know I coulda sneak in if I want to. The newspaper say the women's wing of the Garden overcrowded, and my daddy, Franklin, say is because women go off more often than anyone else. My mamsie, Muriel, say that depends on what you mean by going off. And then Daddy say, who the cap fit, wear it. And then they start to quarrel, and my baby brother, Earlie, start to cry, and I go and sit outside by the side of the house, and count and count the ants marching up the side of the wall.

Later on, after things calm down a bit, Franklin and Muriel undress in the bedroom, and the bed creak, and Muriel cry, and Franklin pant like a dog, and if that's not what you call going off, then I don't know what is. I told Auntie Eileen about this, and she say I getting too big for my boots and too full of mouth. But I was just telling her what I heard, and is not my fault if I hear things. After all, we live in a two-room house with cardboard walls and is hard to keep secrets from a nine-year-old somebody.

Sometimes while Muriel and Franklin carrying on, I walk down the road and peek in at the Garden through the barbed wire fence. There's an ole ackee tree and not much grass, but you should see the periwinkles them—all over! I told Auntie Eileen about the Garden and she laugh and suck her teeth and go out and get me a book bout an English girl with a secret garden. I like to read, and I read the book cover to cover but find not even a mention of periwinkle at all. Auntie Eileen say is because periwinkle really not much better than weeds, and sensible people who really know bout flowers prefer other things like roses and such. I going to stop talk to Auntie Eileen. What she know anyway? The periwinkle's my good-good friends. They grow up close to the fence and we laugh and we talk and they tell me all kind of story bout ole-time days and thing. But you know what? Not a living soul know this excepting me and them and the woman in the window.

Most time when you walk by the Garden you don't see too much of anybody because they keep the women them far from the barb wire on the other side of the yard that face the bay. I hear that they even have a wire fence on that side too, that way the women them won't get a chance to walk out in the sea. Anyway, one time I went by the Garden for a chat and was looking out way-way across the yard, and I see like a woman at a window wave to me. I couldn't make her out good, but it look to me like she had gray hair, heaps of it, and bushy. Don't ask me who it is, I have no idea, but every so often I see her again and we wave and smile and blow kisses. I never did meet my Gran'mamsie. Before I was born she keel over and dead, but I bet she was a nice lady just like that.

Two

MURIEL AND FRANKLIN trying to get visas so us-all can move to New York. Franklin say life too hard here in this piece o' place but maybe if we go somewhere else, we might have a half-chance. Yesterday, Muriel go line up at the 'Merican embassy from six o'clock in the morning. Around twelve o'clock gas fill her up and she feeling sick and she wasn't nowhere near the window yet so she had was to leave. Poor Mamsie. When I grow I up, I going buy her nice clothes and a car and thing and a house with seven rooms! By then I'll be a teacher . . . no . . . a florist. I think I'll be a florist. People will come to my store and the flowers will whisper this and that sweet words in their ear, and they will have to buy the flowers because they will want to hear more.

Muriel went back to the embassy again today. This time they want more papers. She bring home forms to fill out and tomorrow she have to go hustle for this and that signature.

• • •

Muriel say the embassy people they treat her like a dog and she can't say a thing back to them because she well want the visa. Franklin say he going go to the embassy himself and show Muriel how people take care of business.

Franklin come back with his tail between his legs.

I am nine years old and too big for my boots, and if I know how to trace, is because I learn how to trace from Muriel. One time a man try to feel up Muriel in church, and she box him cross his head and trace his family right back to that bad-blood breed of Evans, and if it wasn't for Pastor Olds holding her back, she woulda send the man head rolling all the way to the court house. So why Muriel won't trace out the embassy people them and tell them how to take their little green card straight to hell?

When I grow up I going to buy my Mamsie lipstick and thing, and she won't have to go to anybody embassy to put up with their facety talk and beg them for their little piece o' green card. All those bad-minded people will take one look at her pretty dark lips and they will have to shut up. My Mamsie will say, "This is my daughter—the florist," and they will take one look at my flowers and they will know not to cross my path the wrong way because they will be so fraid that the flowers show them up and trace all their bad blood right back to where it really belongs.

Three

THE OTHER DAY I listen a show on the radio, one of them show where the people them call in and ask question, and I hear a woman call in and say she need a age-paper but she not sure when she was born and she don't know where to get one. This get me thinking, so I ask Muriel if I have one and she say, Yes, then I ask her if I can see it and she say, Later. Anyway, I wait and wait and later never come, so when Muriel and Franklin gone to work I go and root up in their draw. The good thing is, when I ready to root up I never have to fraid that they will come catch me because the two of them work all day sun-up to sun-down. Franklin do yard work for people way across town, cutting their grass and mowing they lawn and thing, and Muriel do domestic work and when she not doing domestic work; she sell in the market. Poor Mamsie, sometimes I feel sorry for her, how she is tired when she come home at night.

Anyway, I root up in the draw and I find a big brown envelope with three piece of paper in there, two of them old and wrinkle-up but one of them fresh and new—I see Franklin's name, I see Muriel's name, I see my baby brother's name, but I don't see my own on any of them. Then I root up some more under the good sheets and towels them that Muriel keep for best and under the nightie that my Gran'mamsie give her, and I see another smaller envelope mark: Gracie-mae Sanders. I open this envelope and a whole heap o' dry-up leaves and dry-up flowers in there and I was bout ready to touch them, but same time the whole of them spill out all over my lap and onto the floor like they was there just waiting to bust out on me. And then I hear like someone humming out by the back door, and quick time I scrape up all the flowers them and seal up back the envelope and put it away in the draw.

Four

IS BEEN ALMOST ONE year now Muriel and Franklin hustling for a visa, and guess what? Yesterday Muriel come dancing in the yard, laughing and wheeling and carrying on: "We get through! We get through!" So last night we had curry and rice and thing and Auntie Eileen buy soft drinks and bun and cheese and the neighbors them come over and we stay up late, talking and laughing, we belly laugh and carrying on. Then this morning the bad news: I'm to be left here with Auntie Eileen. When things settle they will send for me to join them in 'Merica.

I shoulda know say that Muriel would let Franklin trade me off. I shoulda know say she did love everybody better than me. I shoulda know say she would leave me. All the help I help her around the house and look how she do me. All the love I love her and look how she turn gainst me . . .

I going to hide her shoes so she can't leave me. I going to take my skipping rope and tie up her feet so she can't leave me. Yes, I even going to tear up her passport so she can't leave me. And when she ask who tear it up, I going to sing so loud and so long that I won't even hear her. I going to open my mouth and sing like when spirit take up people in church and I going to fling up my arms and roll on the ground and carry on so that she and Franklin will have to get down on their knees to beg me to stop . . .

(Chil'ren, Chil'ren?
                    Yes, Ma'maa?
Where have you been to?
                    Gran'pa'paa.
What did he give you?
                    Bread and cheese.
Where's my share?
                    Up in the air!
How can I reach it?
                    Climb on a broken chair!
Suppose I fall?
                    I don't care!
Who taught you such manners?
                    The dog!
Who is the dog?
                    You!)

Yes, that dutty Muriel and nasty Franklin will have to just go ahead
and pack my bags and take me with them to keep my mouth shut.

Five

POOR MAMSIE SHE only have one pair of shoes and she work her brain so hard to get the little visa.

Six

MAMSIE HAVE TO GO and round up money now to buy her ticket to go 'Merica. Franklin say him have enough money for his own, so Mamsie better hurry up buy hers or she might get lef same place where she sit down on the verandah. So this is how Mamsie piece-piece the money together:

> She sell the radio and the Formica cabinet and her two gold bangles them. She take out her savings under the mattress from selling tamarind balls and grater cake and coconut drops. She get little money from the church fund. She borrow a few dollars from Sister Harris and she promise her say the first money she get in New York she will send her a cuckoo wall-clock to pay her back. She crochet three nice yellow table runners and sell them to the woman's daughter she wash and iron for. Then she still never have enough, so she had was to borrow money from Mrs. Simmons and promise Mrs. Simmons, say she will send her one of those clap-clap lamp to pay her back. Good thing Muriel did join partner, putting in ten dollars every week, and lucky thing it was time for her to draw a good han' or else I don't know what she woulda do. Then some teacher woman see the yel-

low runners them and like them, so Muriel sell six more, this time blue. Anyway, with all that she still never have enough, so she had was to make more drops and make more tamarind balls and make more grater cake and dry up some calabash and carve them up like purse and bowl and shake-shake and thing and sell them in the market. And that's how Muriel buy her ticket.

I see Mamsie walking up the steps to go in the plane. You should see how she slim down with all the way she have to work her brain to get visa and buy ticket, and you should see how the wind just whipping the dress she borrow from Auntie Eileen around her legs. When she reach the top of the stairs she turn round and look, and even though I far away, way up in the waving gallery, my eyes and hers make four and I let out a scream.

Mamsie, Mamsie, don't leave me. Mamsie, Mamsie, please. Mamsie, Mamsie, I know you love me, Mamsie. I know you only trying to make two ends meet Mamsie, but don't leave me. I beg you, don't leave me, Mamsie. Mamsie, Mamsie . . . Mamsie?

Mamsie!

Free Papers, circa 1838

The periwinkle climb around the woman's feet, up her thighs, across her belly, between her breasts, over her shoulders; they encircle her head, brush against her lips, and hang from her ears as she crumbles the free paper in her hand and swears by all her pain o' heart that she will defy the horizon and find her daughters and her daughters' daughters.

Seven

MY MAMSIE LEFT with water in her eye. My Mamsie left with water in her eye. Cheer up, Muriel; cheer up, gal. Cheer up, Muriel; cheer up, gal. Clap Clap. Clap Clap. Ten, ten, ten, ten. Clap Clap. Clap Clap. Ten, ten, ten, ten.

Over the ocean, over the sea. Over the ocean, over the sea. I love ma Mamsie and ma Mamsie loves me. Cheer up, Gracie; cheer up, gal. Cheer up, Gracie; cheer up, gal. Clap Clap. Clap Clap. Ten, ten, ten, ten. Clap Clap. Jump Jump. Ten, ten, ten, ten . . .

On a windowsill in Brooklyn, pink periwinkle chatter.

Muriel

The little garden lizard is watching from a corner in the sun. After night rain, she is red and brown and black—the colors of moist earth. She rests on the limbs of trees, in the tiny cracks between rocks, she watches from among stones under the house and tilts her head when you pass by. Someone glimpsed her at the Port Authority bus depot in New York. She was wearing a green dress and disappeared quickly into the crowd.

One

DOWN IN THE STREET from where we living, some little girls like to skip rope and make up noise just like you, Gracie. Sometimes I listen them, and I just have to close my eyes and smile. After all these years onion still make my eyes water.

The walls of the little room we live in crack up and dirty, and when I think about it, it no much better than the place we did squat inna back a yard. If I had a little money, I would buy a few tin of paint and paint up the place nice—blue and yellow with a long purple border stretch at the foot. The woman upstairs is from Guinea and she give me a pretty piece of cloth to tie my head with, but I think I might as well hang it on the wall instead—next to all the crochet runners that I carry with me here, since I can't find nobody to buy them yet. That yellow one over there is a pattern they call "pineapple," and then that white one beside it is what they call "snowflake," although it look more like Anancy cobweb to me. Abroad-people wasteful, you see, mi chile! Look this nice-nice lamp shade I find on the street yesterday. After I look around quick and make sure nobody watching me, I wrap it up in a piece of plastic and carry it straight upstairs. Then this morning same place, I find this piece of nylon curtain. It dirty but I going wash it up good and hang it at the window.

• • •

Gracie, one month I here now and I finally find a little night shift job cleaning toilets. It don't pay much but it will help make two ends meet. Franklin work same place as me but he have the day shift, and that way at least one of us always with the baby.

After all these years onion still make my eyes water. Today is my day off and I'm in the kitchen cooking. Your Gran'mamsie use to sit at the kitchen table just like this, you know, chopping onion for the pot and her tears just running like river-fall down her face; she use to always say, Not to worry, a little eye water make the pot sweeter.

Two

GRACIE, RIDDLE ME THIS, riddle me that. Guess me this riddle and perhaps not: A woman have three daughters; all of them born one time and all of them tie up with red string and all of them head black. Is what?

I was born in a place they call Kings Pen, a small district with only a handful of people. There wasn't nothing special bout Kings Pen, but I remember I used to have an old Gran'aunt live there name Miss Leela, and Miss Leela had twelve ackee trees. People use to say that the ackee tree them take turns, and a different one bear every month. So that's how come year-round Miss Leela had ackee.

You can find ackee in New York, you know, but it expensive, and if you should ask me, it not sweet like the ackee home.

This building I work in have thirty-six floors; and is me clean number twenty-four through thirty-six. The thirty-sixth floor is the nastiest. You should see how the women them just leave their sanitary pads same place on the floor. Day time when they in the office they dress up nice in pretty clothes and thing, but I tell you, they have no brought-upsy whatsoever. What does it take to just stretch your arm and put your monthlies in the garbage before you leave?

Lord, I clean so many toilets now that I get to hate the sound of water flushing. Sometimes in the morning when I go home tired, just as I nodding off trying to get little sleep, the next-door neighbors flush their toilet, floooshhh, and I jump up scared as if a mad dog was running me down. That Mr. McKintyre must have run-belly as much as he been using the toilet.

One time one of the toilet up on twenty-six wasn't flushing right so I lift off the lid to see if I could see what wrong and I see a little plastic bottle, look like it have in a kind of white powder. Girl, I shut the lid quick and leave the bottle same place, flush; this New York full of trouble and I staying out of it. One week later, my heart take courage and I look again but the bottle gone. Another time the same toilet tank wasn't filling up, so I lift up the lid to have a look and I find a little pen-knife wrap up in a piece of plastic. I fix the toilet and put back the lid quick as a flash. Flush. Anybody ask me anything, I never see it.

Yesterday morning I dream of dogs barking, chasing after me. I was running through some woods toward the sea, and the dogs them was coming nearer and nearer, and then I heard like a gun shot and I woke up sudden, my heart racing. Mr. McKintyre flushing the toilet!

Night time, the building I clean usually empty—nobody there but the security guards and the cleaners—but every now and then you will have somebody working late in their office. Up on thirtieth someone *always* working late. You pass by a closed door and hear like tap tap tap on a typewriter or you hear footsteps or you hear a low voice on a telephone but you don't see anybody. I don't like it at all. It feel like someone watching me and it make me fraid.

• • •

• • •

I wonder why Mr. McKintyre bowels so loose, eh?

Thursday night, I up on thirtieth singing. I like to sing because it help
pass the time and I like how my voice sail out strong in the empty toilet
them. I sing all the ole-time songs your Gran'mamsie used to teach me,
and sometimes when I singing and the sound echo gainst the tile walls,
is as if the two of we voice join together and we wailing out with power
under the anointing of a strong-strong spirit. Anyway, Thursday I was
mopping and lifting my voice and carrying on my usual way when all of
a sudden I feel like someone come up behind me, and when I turn around
I see a man with his tie loose around his neck stand up in the doorway.

>   He say: Will you shut up? It's two o'clock in the morning
>   and I'm trying to get some work done.
>   I say: So am I.
>   He say: I could get you fired, you know.
>   I say: The only fire you have is the fire up your rass.
>   And I point to one of the toilet with shit floating
>   on top.

Girl, every day I waiting to get the axe but nothing don't happen yet, so
maybe the coast clear. But you know what? Even if I get the axe, I still
wouldn't sorry for what I said. As a matter of fact, if I could do it again,
I would take his face and wallow it in his own filth. Still, anytime I up
on thirtieth I take my time tiptoe around and I clean up quick-quick and
leave.

Thursday night I up on thirty-six cleaning and I see like blood dry up
on the tiles them. I say, hmmm, but I keep on cleaning. Six months I
been working here, and I see all kinds of things in these toilets, so noth-

ing don't surprise me now. Anyway, I get to the last toilet, and the floor puddle up with blood, thick blood like it have little pieces of smash-up liver in it. I look in the toilet, and oh God Gracie, it have in a baby, a tiny tiny little thing no bigger than so. Half of the baby flush down in the toilet and just the little lifeless legs them lef sticking out. I say, Oh God, oh God, what to do, what to do? The baby dead already, there wasn't nothing I could do to save it. So what to do? And that's when the thought come to me, just as sensible as you can image it: But of course, Muriel, cut off the navel string and bury it somewhere safe. Quick time, I run to the janitor's closet and turn it upside down. I find a metal file. I say, No, not good enough, and I search some more. I find a rusty scissors, I say, Uh-uh, no, M'am, and I search some more; next thing you know, I find myself running down to twenty-six and lifting up the lid off the trouble-toilet; thank God, the pen-knife still in there, wrap up in the plastic same way.

Back up on thirty-six, I cut off the navel string best as I could. Part of the string was already too far down in the toilet but I get as much of it as I could hold on to. For a while with the string in my hand I feel a little better and I was breathing easy, but then it dawn on me, Oh God, Muriel what you do now? You can close the lid and ignore little white powder inna plastic bottle. You can flush away people filth and throw away their sanitary napkin. But what you going do with a baby? And that's when I decide to tell the supervisor when he come around in the morning.

I get home late that morning. The floor manager ask me question. The police ask me question. The newspapers ask me question. Little most I think they was going to examine me to see if is me do it to my own flesh and blood. The whole time they questioning me I was fraid they would search my purse and find the navel string wrap up in a garbage bag. And what could I say then? And then I remember the pen-knife and the bloody finger prints that I leave on the trouble-toilet on twenty-six, and my mind start to think on all kinda bangarangs that I could get into.

You don't know how I was happy when them let me go. I take the train straight home, right away. When I get there, Franklin was on his way out and I tell him what happen, but I never tell him about the navel string.

Soon as he leave, I take the baby string and bury it in a big ole flowers pot the Guinea lady upstairs did give me. The flowers pot empty—only dirt in there right now—but later I going find something nice to plant put in there. Is the least I can do for the poor little soul.

Three

YOU SHOULD SEE the place now, how little by little I fixing it up. Nobody still don't buy any of the crochet runners but I make two more anyway—this time purple and in a pattern they call "star apple." I had them hanging up with tacks on the wall. Then one day when I was out walking, I find these two nice picture frames on the sidewalk—nice wood frames—and I take them home and polish them up and then I get an idea to frame up the crochet runners inside the wood frames. Oh Gracie, you should see them. I take a piece of black cardboard and make a background inside the frames and then I stretch out the purple crochet on top of it and, girl, you should see how the star apples ripe and pretty hanging up on the wall.

Me and Franklin quarreling every day same way, Gracie. Maybe now it only worse. Is a good thing I don't hardly see him anyway; most time when he come home in the evenings we eat dinner and then I have to get ready quick to go to work for seven.

. . .

Gracie girl, I get so excited with the star apples them that I take one of Earlie ole diapers (he out of diapers now) and I buy up some color thread and I doing little embroidery. The lady upstairs see what I doing and she get excited just like me and she give me two small bamboo frames and I going make up two picture and put one on the wall and send the other one to you.

Anyway, is four o'clock and your baby brother bawling and Franklin soon come home with him hungry belly, so I better put away the sewing for now and go put pot on the fire.

Four

YOU NEVER GUESS what. Yesterday evening Franklin come home and say they have a drug bust on fourteen and they arrest two of the cleaners. Lord have mercy, I hope Franklin don't go and get himself mix up in any foolishness, you know.

Gracie, situation here not too good for me to send for you right now. Life in America hard, and the only milk and honey I find so far is the milk and honey in my heart. Maybe you better off staying same place with your Auntie Eileen. Auntie Eileen have a good job at the post office and she will take care of you. What you think of that? Mmm? After all these years onion still make my eye water.

When you get summer holiday, tell your Auntie Eileen to take you to country to visit your cousins them. I going draw a map for you, and I want you to go to Miss Leela ole yard and find the twelve ackee trees.

I in the kitchen chopping onion. This morning on the way home, I stop at the store and get a half pound of cornmeal. Your Gran'mamsie use to say if all you have is a handful of meal, and a little scrapsy this and that, you can always turn it over with you han' and add little salt and add little water and use you heart and fix it up sweet and set it out nice on the plate and you will never hungry. After all these years onion still make my eye water . . .

• • •

(Earlie! What wrong with you? Ok now, stop the bawling, nothing wrong with your Mamsie. She only chopping onion.)

Gran'aunt Leela, my Granny (on my mother side) sister, use to tell me say it was twelve of them girls in the family. In those days people use to have plenty-plenty pickney; Lord have mercy, I wonder how they use to manage it, eh? My Mamsie tell me that Great-Gran'mamsie twelve baby them was for four different man (Miss Leela never mention that part). Anyway, Miss Leela say that after each one of them born, Great Gran'mamsie plant an ackee tree and bury their navel string under it, and that's how come the twelve ackee trees come in the yard.

When I was a little girl I use to wonder which one of the tree them was growing from outta *my* Granny navel string, but by this time she was already dead and gone and nobody never know. Miss Leela say all she know is that her own string bury on the west side, over by where you walk to go to Marse Percy yard.

I use to go poking around the tree roots them, looking to see if I could find any clues. My Mamsie told me that Granny was a tall thin woman, so I decide say the tallest, skinniest ackee tree would have to be Granny own, but when I check it out, all the tree them was tall and all of them was skinny, so that never tell me nothing. Still, I keep on playing in Miss Leela yard. I use to like to talk to the trees them and I use to put my ears to their bark and listen, just in case Granny call me. There was a kind of special feel about that yard. I use to feel safe there, like the ackee tree them build a fence round me and as if them know me and love me. After a while I get to understand each tree separate. I look at the bark them and I see that each one of them have a face and all the face them long and twist up; sometimes their mouth wide like they laughing a good belly laugh, or their eyes all squint up like they in prayer and supplication, or their mouth poke out and their eye cut, and you know say if the limb them could kimbo they woulda do it.

They used to have a woman in the district name Miss Ida. Miss Ida was a keep-to-herself funny kind of soul, and any time she pass in the street, us children use to laugh and run from her. They use to say that if you and Miss Ida eyes make four, she could put a spell on you. Anyway, one time I was in Miss Leela yard playing with my baby doll and putting her ears to the bark of one of the tree them, and when I look up who should I see looking down at me from over the bougainvil-lea bush? Miss Ida! Girl, I was so scared, I couldn't even run. But when I look good, and me and she eyes make four, I see that Miss Ida face dry and twist up like one of the tree bark them and I see that she couldn't mean no harm. Miss Ida beckon me to come nearer and I step forward little and she beckon me again and I step forward little more and she stretch out her arm and hand me a calabash about the size of a bread-fruit and say to me in a soft-soft voice: Listen. They in there.

When Miss Ida leave I drop the calabash quick time and run for my life, and I stay away from Miss Leela yard for weeks because I didn't know what to make of all of it. When I finally go back there, I see the calabash same place where I leave it under one of the ackee tree them. By this time the calabash was fill up with dirt and grass growing out of it. I bend down closer to look and I hear someone call my name, Muriel, right up close to my ears—a nice sweet voice, like someone that love you. I look around but I never see nobody, so I never answer and I bury the calabash under the ackee tree and that was the end of that.

I wonder what happen to Miss Ida now? The last I heard she was being a nuisance in town and they had to lock her up, poor soul.

Five

THE DAY AFTER I FIND the baby, they had the story in the paper: "Janitor Finds Newborn in Toilet." The newspaper call me "Maureen" instead of Muriel, and then to add coal to fire, they say me is "likely an illegal alien" and I never like that at all, so I call them up and tell them say I don't like how they write me over, and they hang up on me.

Anyway, is been six weeks and I don't hear anything else, so I suppose the police still don't know who the baby belong to, but I bet they drop the case now anyway.

Here is the map to find your way around. Remember Miss Leela tree is the one over by where you walk to go to Marse Percy, and the one over by the bougainvillea is where I did drop and bury the calabash Miss Ida give me. I don't know who live in Miss Leela ole house now since she dead, but that's the house your Gran'mamsie and your Great-Gran'mamsie born in. That house see plenty-plenty hurricane and it still standing. And those ackee tree full nuff-nuff plate and them still bearing. One of them (I think is the one closest to the house) have a little 'Nancy mark into it; look for it, is me carve it with a pen-knife when I was a girl. I know your Auntie Eileen don't fancy ackee, but I going write and tell her to make sure she cook ackee, give you; and don't forget Miss Leela yard have plenty ceracee and mint (look behind the kitchen and around the old chicken coop); take some back to town with you—them good for belly ache. And while you're there, make sure you get some good chocolate tea, not that funny stuff they tin and sell in all the supermarket them. Kings Pen is a cocoa district, cocoa everywhere. Get someone to help you pulp it and wash it and spread it and dry it and heat it and stir it and husk it and pound it and mound it and grate it. The work will do you good.

As you leave the yard to go over by where they call John Crow Railroad, you going see a tall-tall coconut tree leaning to one side—that's your Gran'mamsie, my mother, coconut tree. Make sure you get one of the green coconut and drink it; coconut water good for the heart and you not too young to have bad heart. I hear say if you climb that coconut tree, you can see far-far, way out cross the hill them and over the sea. When your Gran'mamsie string bury under it, everybody say she was going be a traveler and she was going roam far; maybe that's why she did end up leaving country and go live in town, and even after she leave town and go back to country, her mind was always somewhere and elsewhere.

And maybe that's why she don't know where my string bury, because when she have me she was living in a little mash-up place, and she almost dead birthing me and you know how town people stay—nobody couldn't tell where my string bury or if it bury at all.

Now you, Gracie, born in a big town hospital. When the nurse put you in my arms and I ask her for your string, she say they already "dispose" of it. That thing hurt me so much, I call for the doctor but the doctor wouldn't come. And when the doctor wouldn't come, I make up such a fuss that them give me medicine on the sly to quiet me down. I wake up next morning and I bawl so loud, you would think is me just born instead of you. How they think they can just "dispose" of people things so? After all these years onion still make my eyes water. If we don't watch out good, Gracie, all of we beads just going slide off we string and scatter . . .

Six

THE STRANGEST THING happen this afternoon. Earlie was sleeping and I was in the kitchen sitting at the table thinking on this and that when I get the feeling that something funny going on. I get up quiet and go peep through the crack in the door, and when I look, I couldn't believe it—the pot in the corner that I plant the baby string inna full up of periwinkles! Girl, I never see periwinkles big so, and the purple part in the middle of them just looking out at me like eyes. At first I think maybe is the Guinea lady upstairs leave these flowers for me while I was at work and I never did notice them, but when I look, good God, Gracie, the flowers them start to multiply right in front of me and full up the pot even more.

I get down on my knees and take a closer look and it look to me like the flowers them brushing up against their one another and playing with their one another, and when the pot full and couldn't hold no more they start to lean over the side, and I never know periwinkle to be a crawling plant but these start to crawl up the walls, girl, and they never stop till they reach the windowsill. I put my hand to my mouth and I say to myself, *rhaatid*.

Bella

This bend in the river, covered with overgrown bamboo,
could easily be lost and forgotten. Every now and then,
planes in the distance cut the sky, and the periwinkle
wonder, Who is leaving? Down below, tall grass bends
backward and forward,

                                        this way and that way . . .
    Listen to the beating of the partridge hearts
the little lizard hearts   the heart of the mule grazing
at the edge of the river

                                        the mongoose heart
the thin dragon-fly hearts   the heart of old
Mrs. Simons watching from her cardboard shanty on the hill.

    What if, for one moment, we all heard each other?

One

WHEN I WAS LITTLE, my Mama, Anna, use to pull my leg and say: Remember your laughter, and when you eat guava, don't swallow the seeds because they might take root and grow in you. I was so scared, I took her warning to heart, and I watched out for melon, paw-paw, sweet sop, pomegranate, cherry, or any other slippery little seeds that might slide down my throat.

For a long time now, I've had a tiny ball of sorrow which I keep turning over and over in my mouth. I move it around with my tongue and keep it snug for a while under the flap of gum which partially covers one of my wisdoms; then I push it to the front of my jaw into the space behind my lower lip and around and around like that, pausing to chew on it a little but never swallowing it. This sorrow tastes a bit like a piece of cow fat—the sort that sticks to ox-tail bone and is hard to chew. In the morning I wake up and the sorrow is still there; I brush my teeth and rinse my mouth but it hides deep in secret places. I cut a piece of straw from my broom and use it to pick the sorrow out, but then I start to play with it again and I really want to just spit and get rid of it, but it's as if I can't. It stays in my mouth all day like an old piece of something gone tasteless and dry. Perhaps I could swallow it, but what might happen to me then? I would grow fat as a wild calf and become sorrow itself.

Two

YEARS AGO (at the beginning of my second-chance life) I used to be young and beautiful. I had just been reborn from the bowels of the sea; my hair was thick and my legs strong and I had skin that shone in the moonlight like a copper penny. This skin was a special type of skin because I could peel it off whenever I wanted to and be free of it. Nobody knew about this secret except me, and even after I was married, I never told my husband. At night when the houses were asleep, I would creep out to the yard, shed my skin, and leave it under a tree; then I would go down to the river, lay my spirit soft as baby-laugh over the water, and be carried away. The river would take me to all the houses, joy unspeakable, that had newborn babies and I would breathe on the babies and kiss them and whisper sweet things they need to remember. Sometimes the babies would wake up and laugh and the mamas would peep to see what going on but they would never see nothing but moon stretching cross the room or a little moth sleeping on the wall. Then there were nights I would peel off my skin and the breeze would take me up sweet as queen-of-the-night pollen and I would dance from one end of the island to the other, making shadows on the children's windows—hush, hush, hush, hush.

This went on for many years, and every time I took off my skin and put it back on, I became more and more beautiful. I was so lovely that whenever I smiled, little lights twinkled along the creases around my eyes, and my husband started to become worried and nervous, fearful that someone might steal me away. Nights, he tossed restless in bed, putting a chair behind the door and locking me in, so I put a little oil-o-mek-yu-sleep in his tea, slipped out of my skin, and left. In the morning I would be laying right beside him, my breath sweet as jasmine. I got up and ground the cocoa and made the tea and cut the bread and swept the floor and emptied the chimmy and fed the hogs and milked the cow and washed the clothes and spread the white ones in the sun to bleach and shelled the peas and watered the periwinkles, all the while singing . . . and no one knew my secret. My husband watched from the corner of his eye and my skin twitched, longing for night.

One time I came home in the before-day, I had stayed out longer than I meant to and I quickly picked up my skin from under the poinciana tree where I left it, unfolded it, and put it— Ai eeee!!! That Evan, the scamp, had discovered my secret and sprinkled salt and hot pepper in my skin! I burned red hot and rolled around and around in the grass until I became a ball of fire. My blood boiled within me and I felt myself surged along by the wind, burning yellow, burning blue, burning red, rolling and burning, rolling and burning.

Now you know how bad news spreads quickly; nights now when people glimpse my ball of fire, they get all afraid and cover up their children and start to pray. Only the river remembers who I really am. In the wee hours of the morning I go there and soak myself long and well, and then I go home quickly and wrap my raw body in strips of muslin. In this way I get some sleep and receive temporary relief but by mid-day the cloth starts to singe and by sundown I am all ablaze.

Meanwhile, the little ball of fat cooks in my mouth. I turn it around and around—under my tongue, above my tongue—it never disappears. My skin lays withered in a corner under the bed. It has shrunk now and no longer fits. Here is my concern: Before my skin was seasoned by my husband, I discovered a baby girl growing inside of me. That morning when I caught fire and rolled on the grass, she rolled right with me—

a burning wheel within a wheel. I heard her cry, Mama! Perhaps even now, it is her dead flesh I chew.

When I was little, my Mama, Anna, use to pull my leg and say: When you eat guava, don't swallow the seeds because they might take root and grow in you. Today, before sundown, I'm going to spit out this sorrow. I'll go down to the river and breathe deep and gather strength into my lungs and quickly let it go . . .

Claudia

Pig ask her Mooma, "Wha mek yu mouth so long?"
Pig Mooma answer, "Yu a grow, yu will learn."

One

TWICE A WEEK, on Fridays and Saturdays, I do volunteer work at the Garden. So many people congratulate me on the good work I've been doing, and on how generous of me it is to offer up my time like this, that now I feel guilty. The truth of the thing is, I didn't come here because I have a big social heart or anything like that; I came here to find my mother. My mother's name is Lucy. She had me when she was fourteen years old, so that would make her around forty now. Nobody knows where she is; after she had me she got in with a bad crowd in town and disappeared. At one time, rumor had it she was a whore, and then after that, people say they use to see her on the street, sleeping on this and that corner or walking around with a hungry look in her eye. I've been searching for my mother years now; I come to the Garden to look for her because I know that they like to put people away in here when they don't know what else to do with them.

I was raised by Reverend and his wife. They were good people and they treated me like their own, but they were both sickly in old age and nobody wasn't surprised when they dead last year—Reverend in February and Mother P. following him in July. They sent me to school and I took up art. Mother P. used to say, what all this art foolishness you take up? You must be think you is white people pickney. But Reverend always say, leave her go on, mek her draw her little picture them if it make her happy. So I keep on drawing my little picture them, and when I'm not volunteering at the Garden, I teach at the High School.

Years now, I have a recurring dream about my mother. I dream she's laying on the sidewalk somewhere downtown. Her dress is hauled up and her legs spread open. There's all kinds of thick blood and thing running down her thighs, and her eyes are rolled back in her head. People pass by and look and skin up their face, but then they all turn their heads and no one helps her. I want to run to her. I want to scream, Mama! But the word doesn't come out; every time I try to step forward it's as if there are big arms closing around me, holding me back, and then I wake up reaching out into the dark, grasping air.

This dream reminds me of a thing that happened the semester I spent in Missouri. I was walking around, browsing, when a doll in a gift-shop window caught my eye. The price-tag hanging from her foot was marked thirty-five dollars. She was simple, made of black cotton which had been stuffed up fat, and she was wearing a tie-head, a long gathered skirt, and a white blouse. She had two large eyeballs rolled up to the sky; strings were attached to her head, arms and legs, and she hung in midair, next to another puppet—a circus clown. I looked at her for a long time—one leg up, the other down, her arms outstretched, her head tilted at an uncomfortable angle—and such a feeling of recognition came over me.

I began to feel light headed, you know, all dizzy-like, and that's when the door slammed as someone went inside the store, and the dolly's eyeballs rolled forward—for one little instant making four with mine before they settled down at the bottom of their sockets. I pushed the glass door open and I went inside.

Little bells chimed.

There was nothing to be gained from buying her, so I took my penknife, slit the strings, and walked out.

Two

SO FAR I'VE HAD no luck at the Garden. Each month I wander from ward, to ward, but there's no Lucy on any of the admissions lists and many of the women can't remember their names anyway. Still, I feel there's a good chance she is here . . . or may turn up here. What's there to lose?

If it wasn't for the periwinkles, this place would be no more than a run-down tenement yard. The wooden buildings are all rotten and broken and in need of paint, and there are little mounds of trash swept into this and that corner where mawga dogs from the street come poking their noses. To the far south, there's a laundry shed, and next to that, a grassy spot where clothes and linen are laid out to dry. Sometimes while the washer women spread their towels in the sun, I hear them complain to them one another on how many pee-pee spread and dutty wash cloth they have to leave soaking in bleach everyday and how they not getting paid right and how they would leave to rass if they could only find better work. A few yards away there's a kitchen, a storage and garbage room as well as flies (Jesus, the smell!) and more bang-belly dogs and stray cats; then on the opposite side, to the north, are the administrative buildings and a parking lot with trees painted white at their bottoms; a circular drive-way leads to the main entrance where the security guard, Mr. Cameron, is usually half-sleep. Between laundry and administration are the wards—funny little leaky buildings forming a large three-sided plaza. Out in the yard, a skinny ackee tree leans, bending over backward, and after that the land swoops under the barbed wire fence, on and on . . . out to the sea.

Every month when I come here, I look hard in the women's faces, but none of them look like me and all of them look like me. Last year I did volunteer work at the women's penitentiary across the bay and it was the same thing. Some of the women were in there for murder, some for manslaughter, theft, prostitution, "disturbance of the peace"—every sort of crime you can think of. Just as I would begin to think to myself: No, my mother, bad as things may have been, would never do a thing like that, would never talk nasty like that, would never look mash-up and ole like that . . . one of them would glance at me, her face set like a flint and with such hurt in her eyes that I would change my mind right away and search a little longer. In the end, I left the penitentiary only because I had to. The head warden told me that the prison was overcrowded, and so the room usually used for crafts and things like that was being renovated and changed to cells.

Here at the Garden, the women like to make fun of themselves. There's one woman who goes around singing, *tick tock, tick tock*. The other women call her Ms. Tick or Luna Tick but Ms. Tick just laughs and keeps on singing, dancing a little dance by the barbed wire. Then someone adds, usually one of the older women, *trick shock, trick shock*, and after that, there's such a belly-laughing and carrying on that I have to giggle myself. Maybe my mother has a sense of humor.

But then there are times when the yard is quiet-quiet. The women watch the horizon and hum to themselves. Someone snoozes under the ackee tree. Another one cries softly. An old woman walks around, picking up bits of thread, an old chicken bone, and hair from someone's comb—pushing it all in her bra.

Most of the time, at least some of the women seem happy to see me. The crafts room is adjacent to the cafeteria and I go from ward to ward reminding the nurses of my arrival. Usually I end up with a group of at least twenty. Some of the faces change every month, which is good because I need to get a chance to see them all. If I find my mother, I don't know how, but I believe I will recognize her and she will recognize me. I am raking this island with a fine-toothed comb—every tenement yard, every back o' wall, every hill and gully—and if my mother is alive, as God be my judge, I will find her.

When I was twelve and had my first period, Mother P. gave me a note that Mama had left the night she wrapped me up in a piece of flour bag and put me in the hammock on Reverend's verandah. *Dear Claudie,* no one else ever called me Claudie, *if you ever know how inside of me bruck up and if you ever know how I feel shame to leave you like this on Reverend veranda. Take this little kurchif. Use it wipe your nose. Is me stitch it up nice with color thread and thing when me was still in school.* To this day, I never go anywhere without the little kerchief. That Tuesday when I saw my blood, the calico kerchief became my Bible and my treasure map. I was convinced the kerchief contained a clue as to where I might find my mother—I studied it and dreamed it. I sniffed it and rubbed it. I talked to it and prayed to it. One time Billy Graham came to the island and preached at the race course, and he said anyone with a prayer request should send a donation and a clean hanky and he would pray and fast over it and invoke the help of the Lord. But not even Billy Graham could part me and the kerchief Mama made with her own two hands. Besides all that, I lived with a Reverend and I knew first hand about how these things go, so I wasn't so impressed. (I'll tell more about that later.)

Anyway, here is Mama's kerchief. It's hand-hemmed all around with neat little stitches. I can just see her now—thread in, thread out. Then stitched around the inside border, there are tiny red x's, and then a row of purple chain stitch and then another row of red x's. In each of the four corners there's a little leaf, back-stitched in black, with red veins. The leaves are joined together by another row of purple chain stitch, and if you look at these leaves from a certain angle, they look like eyes or sometimes like flames. During class, I used to imagine all kinds of things—my mother's eyes full of fire as I drew the pattern over and over around the margins of my exercise books. And then I started to make up patterns of my own and I decorated all my note books that way—little wiggly flowers and faces growing out of the margins and spreading across the page.

Three

THE FIRST FEW WEEKS I came to the Garden, I brought needles and thread and scraps of cloth and things, whatever I could find; I didn't know what to expect and I didn't know what the women might be interested in. Last year when I worked over at the women's prison, I discovered that the inmates mainly wanted to talk; I'm good at listening, so I didn't really mind. But then some of them started begging me to contact their relatives and children, and I began to realize their true interest in crafts and I saw that we were really all in the same ole pot. Gradually things began to get more and more complicated: This one wanted a flask of rum, please; and that one wanted a little jack-in-the-bush . . . and please, Claudia, if you could only find my baby-father sister, I know she would help me get out of dis piss hole to rass, and, please, I'm begging you to contact my Auntie in the country, long time now I don't hear from her and is she get me in this trouble in the first place with her conniving-self so she better show up with her snake face or else is going be hell to pay; and, please, little sister, don't forget to go to August Town and tell my children I'm alright. These requests were all made as we sat weaving baskets and hats and fans out of pretty color straw to be sold by the prison to craft markets and tourists. The women were not happy about this arrangement, they thought they should be entitled to receive at least a portion of the money for them-

selves, but they kept on coming to crafts anyway because they wanted
to find their Aunties and Grannies and because they needed a little
white rum to keep on going. So this is the mess I was pulled into. I
found myself making trips to Jones Town and this and that town and
district. I was getting in deeper than I could swim. Sometimes I just had
to say, No, I can't do that, but then there were times when one of them
would look at me with eyes as old as flints and how could I refuse?

So when I first came to the Garden, I didn't know what to expect.
The women eyed me up and down, reading me all over. Some of them
just stood with their backs against the wall, refusing to sit down. But I
soon found out that among them there were many who were bored and
eager to put their hands to use. The first box of scraps I brought was
used up quickly, transformed into hooked rugs and quilts and little
lizards filled with John Crow beads. None of them even needed me to
tell them what to do. I put the materials on the table and they took over
right away—cutting and stitching, cutting and stitching. Thread in,
thread out. So I have to admit I've learned a thing or two in this Garden.
This month we worked on straw, and one woman, Ida, made the most
beautiful mats, patterns spiraling without end into loops and circles.
She says she learned to weave when she was a girl growing up in the
country. Next month she wants me to bring some gourds. I can't wait
to see what she'll do with them.

Reverend was a good father, but let me tell you something, he was
crooked. He used to make like he was prophesying but he couldn't see
into the future a damn lick. The district we lived in was small, and the
vestry used to double as the post office. Reverend used to steam open
people's letters and read all their business, and then he used to get up
on the pulpit and preach how the Lord came to him in a vision and
revealed a family in our midst who is going to be visited with a great and
terrible tragedy. After the sermon everyone would march up to the
altar, wondering if it was them and praying that it wouldn't be, and

Reverend would take a bit of olive oil and anoint their foreheads, and everyone would in the name of Jesus make sure they paid their ten percent tithe and their ten percent offering. Then Monday morning when the vestry turned post office, someone would get the news that their son abroad got locked up for shooting a man in a gas station, or that their granddaughter got run over by a pick-up truck, or that the test from the doctor in town came back positive. There would be a big hollering right there on the vestry steps and everyone else would hear it and breathe a sigh of relief. Sometimes Reverend got his prophesies from listening out for good bits of news that most of the congregation who were either too poor or too old might not be privy to. Like the time he said the Lord had shown him a sign of the heavens in turmoil, filled with falling stars, a warning that the lukewarm and sleepy had angered the Lord and they should repent or be spewed from his mouth. All week everyone stayed up watching the sky, and sure thing on Friday night there were stars falling this way and that—Reverend had anticipated the event by keeping up with subscriptions to the *Astronomer's Newsletter.*

I was always a step ahead of Reverend and that's how I knew all of this. One morning I caught him opening letters, and after that I began keeping an eye on him, browsing through his magazines, watching his comings and goings, keeping an ear open to his telephone conversations. Mother P. didn't know any of this, or at least she pretended not to. She said Reverend had prophesied that a child would be discovered, left for dead within their midst, and the next month I was found— sucking my thumb on the verandah.

Four

BIG HEADLINES IN THE newspaper this morning: There's been a riot at the women's penitentiary. A building was set on fire, apparently to distract the wardens. One woman escaped and three were gunned down, climbing under the barbed wire. No identification of the dead, but there's a picture of the woman who got away. The papers say she could be armed and dangerous. In the mug shot her eyes glitter with mischief and I immediately like her. I picture her stalking off to the hills, a razor blade hidden under her tongue.

Later in the Garden the women were restless. Luna paced back and forth, muttering, and Mrs. Johnskin was crying, her arms, palms forward, raised up to the sky. Two women were under the ackee tree quarreling—tracing off the nurses to dutty hell. I had to laugh to myself. It's true that Nurse Watson's breath smells like a fowl coop. Sometimes I avoid her just so I won't have to smell it.

Then on the evening news they had more on the prison story, and I began to wonder about the dead all shot up under the barbed wire. I thought how maybe one of them could be somebody I promised a favor—someone who wanted to get a message to their Granny or sister. And then a wave of something came over me and I started to feel so shame for not doing more, but more than that I was angry at the guards for shooting down people like wild hogs on the run.

Meanwhile, the escapee, Myra, a.k.a. Prickle Fern, is still at large. The news people say she was a known trouble-maker. On several occasions she had been picked up by police for haggling tourists on private beaches, lounging in hotel lobbies and refusing to leave, then finally in a brawl with an Englishman (concerning the beach bag on his deck chair,) she drew out a pen-knife and slashed his lip. The Englishman was Sir Somebody-or-Another, and it made big news here and bad press abroad.

I turn off the T.V. and climb into the bed. I close my eyes against the darkness and I urge Fern on. I dream of dogs, so many of them, barking barking barking, chasing me through the trees, and all the way to the beach.

Five

FROM THE MOMENT Mother P. found me on the verandah it was heaven come down and glory fill her soul. She had been trying to have a baby for years but without success; people said she was a mule. So no second thoughts, she knew right away that if the mother didn't turn up, she would get papers and keep the baby.

I grew up hearing this God-works-in-mysterious-ways story over and over. Everyone agreed that I was probably Lucy's baby, that streggae who went and got herself pregnant only-God-knows-where and then dropped it like a pup and took off and disappeared. The story was always left at that: Mother P. didn't want to spoil her miracle with too much thought, and according to Reverend, the Lord's book was already sealed. But for all Mother P.'s love, I couldn't forget Lucy, and by the time I was around eleven and had caught on to the real wind inside Reverend throat, I knew there had to be something else behind my appearance. I mulled it over for a couple of years, I looked at Reverend's nose and I looked at mine, and it didn't take long to put two and two together and realize, ahem, Reverend found himself in some mess with this young girl and tried to resolve it up nice.

I never did confront Reverend about any of his "prophesies" but toward the end of his life they became less and less frequent. Doctor said he had a growth in his stomach as big as a dry coconut. He became slow and distracted, always looking off in the distance. He stayed inside all the time, barely able to hold down his food until he just withdrew to the bedroom and never came out again. I remember watching him lying on his death bed, his eyes all glazed over with a thing just like cow cream as if he was blind. Suddenly I got scared, I wanted him to talk to me, to say something quick. I whispered, Reverend! Reverend! and he answered me all broken and weak-like, Yes, Lucy. Yes.

So it looks as if Fern has outwitted the police dogs. She's nowhere to be found. Perhaps the German shepherds have all returned with their tails between their legs. And I bet somewhere out there she's sharpening her pen-knife, and smiling.

Six

So THIS MONTH WE START gourd work at the Garden. Miss Ida, bless her heart, is the queen of gourds. I went to the country and picked a whole basket full and bought them here, and of course, she took over right away. I brought all my carving tools with me and offered them to her but let me tell you, Miss Ida didn't want any of that, she prefers to work with her pen-knife and a piece of glass bottle. She and the other women carve up bowls, pots with lids, plant hangers, savings boxes, little purses, handbags, shake-shake rattles—oh, you should see all of it!

I brought some home to show the girl I share apartment with, Sharon. Sharon and I met at university; that was a long time ago but she's still not finished yet because her thesis is giving her too much trouble. She has a job at telephone company now and it well suits her because she's always gossiping, a real mout-a-massy. Anyway, Sharon didn't seem to find nothing special in the gourds, she just glanced at them and put her nose back in her work. When Sharon starts to carry on like that, I just kiss mi teeth and let her talk to herself.

But the gourds—you should see them, etched out with all kinds of designs that loop and turn . . . Last night I tossed in bed and couldn't sleep—my mind wandering on this and that—and then one of the patterns came to me, loops spiraling around, wheeling and turning. I traced it with my finger, trying to find the source of it. Outside, rain was coming down all soft-like, pipper-pit pipper-pit pipper-pit, and I felt myself floating. I dreamed my hair was falling as silent as ashes onto a large white plate set in front of me. I put my hand to my head, and thick strands disintegrated like powder between my fingers. Soon my hair was all gone and the plate was full. I heard a soft laugh behind me, heh heh, and I turned around to see who it was—somewhere a door slammed and I woke up to rain blowing in through an open window.

Seven

TODAY WHILE THE women were busy gutting out more gourds, I wandered over to the back window of the crafts room and saw the loveliest little girl standing in a patch of sunlight. She was wearing a ragga-ragga green dress, and with the sun shining like that you could see her little bamboo legs through it; she had her arms stretched out like bird's wings and she was twirling around and around with her eyes closed and she was singing a little song, *Cheer up, Gracie; cheer up, gal.* At first I thought she might be one of the washer women's daughters, but then I remembered that they have half-day off on Saturday, and anyway if they bring their children to work, they could lose their job. The little girl twirled around and around till she fell down on the grass in the middle of the sun spot, and then she took off her shoe and shook it and a piece of paper fell out, and that's when I noticed the periwinkles shifting, all of them tilting their heads toward her, as if they were waiting to hear what's inside the letter. The girl unfolded the paper and read it, and the periwinkles multiplied up closer and closer until they were climbing onto her lap and they made a little circle around her waist. I wanted to call someone and say, Come, look, but the women were still busy gutting out gourds, and I somehow felt silly distracting them. I looked over at Miss Ida and saw that she had been watching me all along, my eyes and hers made four, and when I turned back to the window the little girl was gone.

Over the ocean, over the sea. Over the ocean, over the sea.

Eight

LAWD HAVE MERCY, Miss Ida has an idea. Next Monday is going to be electric shock day, she says, and she wants me to get her and Mrs. Johnskin out of this place and drive them to country before then. I said, But, Miss Ida, you know they not going to let me just take you out like that. But even as I resisted I felt like a hypocrite because I know that nothing's wrong with Miss Ida's head more than anybody else own, and as for Mrs. Johnskin, she belongs with her family or with friends somewhere but not in a place like this.

To tell you the truth, nothing would please me more than to be able to pull it off and get them out of here. But how? The security guard, ole Mr. Cameron, usually half-sleep, that's a plus. And between two and four the nurses usually watch their t.v. show, that's another plus. Then there's the fact that nobody doesn't suspect me anyway. So if I could just get them from the crafts room and past the wards and nurses and then past the administration building to the parking lot, we could all jump in the car and get out scot-free. But how to do it?

All night I lay in bed thinking on this thing. Sharon's boyfriend, Derek, is staying over tonight. I can hear her in the bedroom moaning. This moaning goes on and on till I wonder to myself whether Derek is all that sweet or if Sharon is just putting on a good show. I remember how in the country when they used to kill goat, how the goat used to holler when the throat got slit. I have to give it to Sharon: She slits Derek's throat well.

Nine

OF COURSE I COULDN'T just forget the periwinkles as easy as that. So Saturday I turned up a little early and went and checked out the spot myself and, hah, just as I was coming from behind the crafts building I glimpsed the little green dress disappearing behind the tamarind tree. I went over and looked but I didn't see the girl anywhere and I didn't see where she could have gone to. Perhaps she could have climbed the tamarind tree, but then she would have to jump from there to the other side of the high concrete wall which was topped with broken glass and barbed wire. I looked at the periwinkle but they were still and quiet as if to say, We never saw a blessed thing. I saw an ole rusty wash tub turned upside down on the grass and I kicked it over with my foot, but it was empty and the periwinkle were still silent. I felt like the periwinkle were playing a game with me. I felt like they knew where the girl was and that they were just holding their breath, laughing, waiting to see if I would figure it out, but more than that, waiting to see if I believed in them enough to ask.

I didn't ask.

After crafts I drove home slowly, searching the streets for the little girl but she was nowhere to be found. It started to get late; the street lights

were coming on; the ole bruck-up Rabbit was running out of gas, so I
headed on home.

Ten

ANYWAY, WE'VE WEIGHED this against that, and we're going to take our chances. Friday is school holiday, so I'll be off from work and will go to the Garden instead. A weekday is the best because that's when *As the World Turns* comes on and all the nurses are hooked to it. I'll end crafts at five minutes to three and walk the group back to the wards. By the time they arrive, the show will be just starting and the nurses won't be bothered with checking too much. I've seen them before when their show comes on, all huddled around the t.v.; they turn their backs and don't give a damn who's calling, Nurse, nurse, or knocking a head against the wall. I'll sign out as usual on the notebook by the office door. I'll call, Later, nurse! and the earth will be spinning at such a speed that Nurse Watson will already be on the edge of her chair and she won't even bother to look around, she'll just call back, Later, Claudia! and me and Miss Ida and Mrs. Johnskin will walk quickly to the parking lot. We'll jump in the car, and if Mr. Cameron is too awake and too suspicious, I'll give him a smile and a big tip (everyone knows that a good pay-off goes a long way on this island).

Meanwhile, I have some business to take care of. The periwinkle watch me everywhere I go. It's as if they know my plans and are waiting for me to acknowledge them so they can give me their blessing. So far, I've ignored them—perhaps I've been afraid of what it would mean to admit there's such a thing as magic.

Eleven

ONE TIME MOTHER P. told me broken egg shells good for plants, and look, I have a plastic bag full of crushed shells from a month's boiled eggs. See, I've come to sprinkle them at your roots. I am just an ordinary woman and this is all I have to offer, but take them. Please, take them.

Sun sets orange and the little lizard crawls under the fence and out into the street. She waits under some leaves, tilting her head, watching the feet go by. It's been so long now, and still the periwinkle argue whether she is a woman pretending to be a lizard or a lizard who longs to be a woman. So, after all, there is at least one thing not even the periwinkle know.

Bella

Madda Wilma dressed up in garbage bags

at Half-Way-Tree

has not eaten for days.

      Hunger for revolution has bored a hole

                  through her navel

    and bloated her stomach;

             her eyes

shift back

             and forth,

this way

               and that way,

watching the earth

                  as it whirls

        on its axis

in a frenzied dance

              around frenzied light.

Tilting her head

    at that precise angle which prevents dizziness,

she beckons to school children,

whispering: Come, look. Listen to me, nuh?

The children stop;

jump a little ring-a-ding,

then run, laughing.

Perhaps she could wait instead

for the tiny feet

of the unborn,

but they will arrive

late and even further removed

from the center

of passing memory.

So tonight,

a wheel in the middle of a wheel,

her bloated belly

will explode

into necessary words—

circling   and separating

into half-moons   and blazing lights

enough to stir the bones

of the long-dead

whose dark marrow

seeps deep

into the hidden core of the earth.

In the meantime,

                   there is evidence of disturbed blood:

the twitch of a lip, an eyelid, an ear,

                   and always

                                 coconut trees   leaning

closer to the ground.

Old Mr. Cameron shifts on his stool in the little cubicle by the gate. He reaches for his cane and hums to himself, tapping out a tune. He hears the Rabbit approaching and closes his eyes, then pretending to yawn, he puts his hand to his mouth to hide his smile. It's raining again, God's speed, God's speed . . .

When I was little, my Mama, Anna, use to tell me: Mind what you eat, and when you eat guava, don't swallow the seeds because they might take root and grow in you. Now a ball of sorrow cooks in my mouth and I feel like a mule chewing her cud.

And it's raining again.

I am on my way to spit out this sorrow. Rolling and burning, rolling and burning. This time the river will help me to spit it all out; she is a good listener. During the rainy season her banks are flooded with stories carried by the rain; red clay washes underground and she is dark as war blood. From a distance, the man in the moon thinks she is the whipping red scarf of a woman galloping on horseback. But even he knows, this is not sport—this is war. The voices in the rain go pipper-patter, pipper-patter, as the river charges and roars all the way to the sea.

All day they had been watching and listening. Restless. In the evening it came, a soft hum in a woman's contralto voice, carried from cane blossom to cane blossom, the whole field swaying. No one knew who or where she was, this woman, the source of the hum; her voice moaned and rustled against cane stalks and there were no words, but everyone understood her meaning.

Night came, they waited for lights in the Great House to be put out, and then they stole away into the darkness . . . It was a cloudy night and there were no stars; they huddled together in the woods, waiting for a sign, wondering which way to go. A woman's baby, hidden in her bosom, started to cry. Somewhere a dog barked and they all jumped in fear. We told you not to bring babies. No babies, someone snapped. The woman shoved a withered nipple in the baby's mouth but the baby wailed and wailed, and the woods shook with its wailing. They all saw it at the same time: a ball of fire coming through the trees, burning yellow, burning red, burning blue. It spun around and around, making a winding path, and the baby suddenly calm, whispered, Sweet chariot o' fire. The woman, shocked, stared at the baby because it was only two months old and nowhere near talking. The ball rolled passed the huddled group and they saw that something in its center flapped and blew like so much sorrow. The baby pointed and cooed and they watched the ball of fire spin away, smaller and smaller, a flicker no larger than a firefly.

Afterward, a man bent down to touch the ground; it was hot as a frying pan, and immediately a small cluster of star-like flowers sprung up at the place where he had put his finger. The flowers shone like knowing eyes and began to multiply, marking out a constellation in the woods—here a star, there a star—as if the sky had fallen to the ground; the people followed the twinkling lights, silently, all the way to the hills.

Part Two

Madam Fate

Gracie

Excerpt from *The Long-Ears Woman's Book of Herbs*

Madam Fate *(Isotoma longiflora* [syns: *Laurentia longiflora, Hippobroma longiflora*]*)*
Common Names: Star Flower, Horse Poison, Night-sage
Madam can help you if you are seeking direction or have an old wound; Handle her carefully—she holds life in one hand and death in the other. And remember, she is a private woman; she blossoms by night and doesn't like her name to be called out loud.

One

YESTERDAY WE WENT to the docks to get Mamsie barrel she send from 'Merica. Auntie Eileen was all excited—say she hope Mamsie send the new shoes and thing she ask her buy. The whole time I wait beside Auntie Eileen for the man to bring the barrel come, I praying say, Is really Muriel hiding in the barrel ready to jump out and pop big kiss give me. When we reach home Auntie Eileen quick time grab a knife and start cut around the barrel lid, but before she could even finish open it we hear a tap on the door and when I look I see Mrs. Simmons all smiles come for her clap-clap lamp.

Poor Mamsie, she say she don't find no milk and honey in 'Merica yet, so I wonder is how she manage work her brain to buy all these things? Shoes for Auntie Eileen and clothes and school things for me and the bottom of the barrel full up with a heap o' rice and flour and milk powder. I try on the pretty dress she send for me but I just couldn't hold it in no longer: long eye-water just running down my face and the whole of me shaking. Auntie Eileen say, What a bad-minded ungrateful pickney, eh? But is because she don't know I really miss Mamsie, and I worry for Mamsie up in that cold place where she is with the dutty toilet them.

Mrs. Simmons plug in the clap-clap lamp, and you should see how it sweet her. She laugh and she clap and she laugh and she clap, and you woulda think is Christmas how Auntie Eileen pose-off on the sofa in her new shoes and handbag, eating 'Merican cheese crackers.

I slam the door and I go out in the yard, and same time Mrs. Paul see me in the 'Merican dress and she call through her window, Barrel come? and before I could even answer her she dash outta the house and knocking on Auntie Eileen door.

This dress too full of Mamsie hard work and crosses for me to wear it. Every time I put it on I feel like a ole ole woman. Is not because the dress ole fashion or anything like that, but every time I put it on, eye-water just well up in my two eyes and I just can't stand it. Last Sunday Auntie Eileen say, "I not going church with you looking like a dog-dead-an-lef puppy, so you better go put on the dress or else." I never like how that sound, so I say to her, "You better mind the puppy mother never dead in truth, trying to get you those shoes you pose-off inna." And then she slap my mouth and say I too force-ripe, so anyway, I put on the dress but this time I never cry, I just suck my teeth.

Two

So FAR AUNTIE EILEEN don't know anything about me going to the Garden. Auntie house kinda far from there, but still, if I go a little bit outta my way, I can pass by the Garden on my way from school. Auntie Eileen say the street the Garden on not safe and the only reason she was coming over that way was to visit me and Earlie and Muriel and Franklin. What Auntie say is true anyway: The other day I was walking and a man behind a tree show me his thing and call me with his finger; I was so frighten, I run all the way home. Then last week on that same-same corner, someone get all shot-up in a gun fight. I never see the fight but I see all the police cars and I see the crowd and I push my way through and I see a man lay down on the ground, his face cover up with a towel and the towel all bloody. I stand there watching because I never see anybody so bloody like that before, and a police lady come from behind me and grab my shoulder and she look at me all serious and she say, Little girl, is where your mother?

Anyway, so far Auntie Eileen don't know anything. Evening, by the time she come back from the post office I usually home already. Auntie Eileen rent a place from a family that leave their house to go live over in foreign. She have a bedroom and a kitchen and a shower and it small, but it much more nice than the little shaka-shaka zinc place I did live inna with Muriel and Franklin. Muriel say I should be glad to live with Auntie Eileen because where we was living before even puss fraid to walk, and where she is in New York not much better, either. Auntie Eileen take good care of me but I don't feel for her like how I feel for Mamsie. She have a school teacher boyfriend that come around some-times. You can always know when she talking to him on the phone because she put on a special voice and she laugh all nicey-nicey, not the usual belly-laugh she always have. When he come over she always make sure my clothes change and my hair comb, and I hear her tell him all kind o' lie bout where she born and where she school while I sit down right there next to her knowing goodness well is lie she telling because is right downa Kings Pen she born and grow. See that's the dif-ference between Mamsie and Auntie Eileen. Mamsie don't hardly change up nothing for nobody, but Auntie Eileen now, well, she fright-en for people.

Ole Mr. Cameron, the security guard at the Garden, usually half-sleep, so sometimes if I don't see anyone else, I just sneak right past him and walk quick-quick through the gate. Usually I stay away from where anyone might find me, and I go and play behind one of the old build-ings them where there is plenty grass and plenty-plenty periwinkle. I have all of Muriel's old letters saved up, and I like to take them to the Garden and read them. At first Muriel wasn't believing me bout the periwinkle, but now they growing right there on her windowsill in Brooklyn, so she have to quick time change her tune. The periwinkles like for me to talk to them; they know a heap o' story from way way back what everybody else already forget and we lay down on the grass and we laugh and we talk . . .

One time there was a woman name Taymus that did have a nice-nice silver needle that her Gran'madda did give her before she dead. This needle was a special-special needle because no matter how the cloth favor flour sack or ginger bag, any clothes sew with the needle always pretty and them always fit sweet.

Taymus used to keep the needle lock up high in the top shelf of her Formica cabinet because she never want none of her pickney them lose it and she never want nobody tief it neither. She was a poor-poor woman and sometimes when she go town and come back, is only just a handful of peas or a little cornmeal she coulda afford, but people around the district soon start find out how she good with her needle and them start give her them Sunday dress and thing for her to sew, and even though them was poor themself and couldn't pay her much, that's how Taymus coulda make little money to feed her children.

When the people them bring their cloth for her to sew, she use to lay it out nice and flat on the bed, and then she cut and she sew, and she cut and she sew, and she tap her foot and she sing a little song that she use to hear her Gran'madda sing:

> Time longa dan thread inna needle,
> yes, mi dear.
> Time longa dan thread inna needle,
> yes, mi dear.

Sometimes the song sweet her so much that she get carry away and she forget is almost sundown and is time to put pot on fire for the pickney them dinner. Everybody always please with the clothes Taymus sew give them, and soon the whole district dress to puss backfoot. Morning time, Taymus look through her window, and she see how all the little children them going to school and dress and look nice, and she smile a little smile and she hum to herself:

> Time longa dan thread inna needle,
> yes, mi dear.

Now you know how tongue can fly, and it never take long before news spread how all the people them over River Gully prims off in all kinda fancy style and thing. Some people say the style them come from Henglan' and some people say them come from 'Merica and some people say, No, is Hafrican style River Gully people wearing. Ha, Anancy daughter did well like fashion, and when she hear the news, she say to herself, I *mus* find out is what going on downa River Gully. Quick time she ketch a ride and she go downa Gully, and them tell her say is a widow woman name Taymus mekking the clothes them. Now Anancy daughter was a cubbitious young girl and she wasn't just satisfy with paying Taymus to make her the clothes, uh-uh, she did want to tief Taymus needle. Lord help us.

Ha, Anancy daughter go to Taymus and tell her how she getting married soon-soon and how she well need a nice gown and how she know say is only Taymus can make the gown sweet like how she want it. Taymus say, alright, and Anancy daughter leave out the door and make like she going home but she never leave, she stay there same place hide under the window. Anancy daughter wait and she wait and soon she hear a singing:

> Time longa dan thread inna needle,
> yes, mi dear.
> Time longa dan thread inna needle,
> yes, mi dear.

Anancy daughter peep her head over the windowsill and she see the silver needle dancing like twinkling star between Taymus finger, and she say, Ah ha, that's the trick! and she go on home.

Next week Anancy daughter come back to get her clothes. She put on a nice voice (Ooo lovely!), and she throw arms around Taymus neck thanking her for the gown. Same time while she have arms around Taymus neck sweetening her up, Anancy daughter stretch her hand and tief the needle from outta where it stick in a green mango. Taymus feel like something drain from out the room but she never know is what and she never say nothing.

Heh, Anancy daughter so excite, she go home and quick time she get a piece o' flour bag and she take out the needle and she start to cut and she start to sew. Thread longa . . . Poor Miss 'Nancy, she couldn't member the song . . .

> Thread longa dan time inna needle,
> yes, mi dear.
> Thread longa dan time inna needle,
> yes, mi dear.

Anancy daughter get the song mix up, and the thread start to tangle her up and tangle her up and poor Miss 'Nancy she couldn't move.

Thread longa than time inna needle,

yes, mi dear.

The thread tie her up aroun and aroun a tamarind tree, and she couldn't stand it no longer and she let out a holla, and in the end is her Mamsie hear her and have to come save her. Anancy daughter Mamsie did well vex and she throw up her arms in the air, and she bawl, Lord-a-massy, look how the gal-pickney shame me, tiefing people needle like that! Miss 'Nancy Mamsie beat her and beat her and send her straight back to Taymus with the tiefen needle. Taymus take back the needle and she say, *Yes, mi dear,* just like that.

From that time on Miss 'Nancy Mamsie start to teach her daughter sewings. Miss 'Nancy get so good that she start to make all kinda silk gown and thing, and so many man admire her inna her pretty silk that some of them even lose them soul trying to get inna her clothes. Heh, Miss 'Nancy don't have no time for no fool-fool man, she busy making sewings. So sometimes when you look up in the corner and you see the Anancy rope them hanging there, don't bother use your broom to bruck them down, leave them stay there, them not bothering you—is Miss 'Nancy work her brains and sew them up all pretty-pretty like that, and time longa dan rope.

Three

TODAY IS MY ELEVENTH birthday. Auntie Eileen says I have to try to be a good girl this year because the number eleven can be just like the two sticks in hell. She took me downtown to Sangsters and I picked out a book that I liked. Auntie Eileen says that the book is full of big people business and is too grown for me, but I look at the cover and I see a girl on the front holding her doll baby and the girl woulda almost look like she could be my sister, so it must have something in there that concern me, and even if it don't, I going to keep it and read it later. Then after that we went to get soda and patties and we sit down at the counter and chat and eat, and Auntie Eileen touch my face all soft and say, Look how I growing up with a fire-mouth just like Muriel, and the way how she say it you woulda almost think she sorry for me. Before we leave she take a little brown parcel from out her handbag, and when I see that is Muriel's handwriting on there I start to smile. I pull off the string and unwrap the paper, and I see a nice little bamboo frame with a photo of Muriel all wrap up in her wool hat and winter coat. The picture fix up pretty with the photo glued right in the middle of a nice white crochet; I notice the crochet right away because I know say is Muriel make it with her own two hands. Auntie Eileen look at the crochet and say, Oh look, a snowflake, and I just laugh, heh heh, to myself. Me and Auntie Eileen watch the picture for a long time. Auntie Eileen say, Muriel must be doing well 'cos she look like she gain some weight, but I say, No, is the coat make her look big like that, look at her two little leg them stick out from under it. All the same, Muriel have a big smile on her face, but I know Muriel like how she know herself and I bet you any money she was there shivering in the cold and just putting out her best so she could get a nice picture to send to me.

Anyway, Muriel stick a letter behind the frame and here is the news: things in New York not going well and she still can't send for me yet, so I'm to stay here with Auntie Eileen. Muriel say she can do me more good abroad than what she can do for me here because at least over there she can work little money to send me food and thing so I won't end up like one of them bang-belly streggae you see walking around town. I not vex with Muriel this time, but I feel disappoint. I just hope she not shame to go so far and come back with her two hands empty, poor and mawga same way. Everybody that go abroad talk about how abroad-life hard, but still people running over there and when they go, they don't come back. If things so bad, I think Mamsie should just come on home. But you can't tell Muriel anything, she too one-minded. When I grow up, I going to be a florist. I going to have a nice little flowers shop and I going to buy my Mamsie lipstick and thing, and she won't have to clean anybody's toilet and put up with their nastiness. All day long we going talk to the flowers and fix them up nice in clay pots and thing. When night time come we going drink ginger tea and tell all kinda story, and then we going fall asleep on a big-big soft mattress and I bet you when we wake up in the morning we breath going smell sweet just like jasmine.

So this is the dream I dream over and over: I running through some trees, running running as fast as I can. Some dogs behind me, barking and chasing me. I feel so tired so tired so tired, and just when I think I can't take another step and I about to fall down, I reach the beach and

I see the big sea spread out in front of me. I don't have no choice, and I keep running running straight ahead, right inna the water. The sea cover me up and I feel the warm water pushing me, pushing me far down in one deep-deep sink hole, and when I open my eyes and look, I see a whole heap o' bones scatter at the bottom of the water, little skinny arms and fingers and thing, spread like them all did stretching for something far-far away.

Four

Is SUMMER HOLIDAYS and every afternoon I listen for the sound of the post-man bicycle, ching ching, coming up the road. When I hear it I run out to the gate and most time he just ride right pass me, but some-time he stop and my heart get all happy. Muriel write a couple times a month—I have all her letters saved up under my mattress. Whenever the time come that Muriel send for me, it going to be funny because I already know all bout the people that live in her building. Muriel say she start figure out Mr. McKintyre now: Whenever he let out a belch, that mean the trouble on the way, and you can count it by the clock and bet your last penny on it—half hour later, the toilet going to flush. Then the Guinea lady upstairs introduce her to a friend, and this part is funny: The friend, Andrea, use to go to the same school that Muriel did go to when she was a young girl just move to town. Muriel say the woman face look familiar but she just can't place her.

So, anyway, is summer holidays and I have plenty time to go here and there while Auntie Eileen at the post office. Usually after the post-man come and gone, I put on my shoes and quick time go on down the road. Before I go anywhere I always make sure the post-man out of sight, though, because you never know, maybe he know Auntie Eileen and he really come to check on me. You have to be careful with Auntie Eileen, you know. Sometimes she call in the middle of the day, and if you not at home, you better have a quick tongue and a good story to give her when she come back. Is true, sometimes I go to the library because I like to read and I like how the books them smell and Auntie Eileen don't mind that, but Lord I hope she don't ever find out that I going over the Garden. Over this way is just only houses and everybody stay in them yard, but over by the Garden, things always happening and every day different from the other one. Sometimes I like to just stand up in the street and hear the whole heap o' cuss-cuss and carrying on. When we did live inna the dungle yard, I did have a friend, Tonia, and me and Tonia used to enjoy playing like we is two grown people cussing out wi one another. Sometimes, I use to cut kimbo and trace out Tonia so bad that she start to take it for real and get all vex with me. That's when the game used to get really sweet because Tonia was small but she had a good tongue in her and I knew how to provoke it. I used to say all kinda thing that I did hear Muriel tell people when she tracing them. Sometimes me and Tonia use to play like she is the rich lady and me the house helper, or sometimes one of us would be the baby-mother and the other one her baby-father girlfriend. This used to go on and on till one of us start to laugh or one of us mother call us inside because she don't like what we carrying on with. I don't hear from Tonia for a long time now; her Mama was sick in the hospital, and the last time I saw her she say she was going to live with her Gran'mamsie in the country. Some people say Tonia mother dead from AIDS and some people say she dead from new moania and some people say, No, is obeah, somebody obeah her. All I know is, Tonia mother dead.

Then this afternoon, I get another letter from Muriel. Nothing still don't change; the toilet them dutty same way. Look like she and Andrea turn good-good friends, though. Sometimes the two of them go walking in the nice 'Merican stores and they try on all kinda pretty clothes—just to see how they look because of course they can't afford any of it. Muriel say one time she and Andrea was in the dressing room trying on clothes when all of a sudden two piece o' sponge fall outta

Andrea brassiere. Poor Andrea, Muriel say she had cancer and doctor had to cut off her two titty.

The periwinkle tell me a story bout a woman that had two titty that grow so long, they reach all the way down to her knees. This woman name was Auntie Nora. Auntie Nora had plenty-plenty pickney and all of them born one after the other, and as soon as they born they reach for her titty and that's how come the titty them turn long like that. The periwinkle say sometime the other woman them use to laugh after her, but Auntie Nora never pay them any mind, she just hold her head high and take one of her titty and fling it over her shoulder like say is a silk scarf or thing, and then she smile a little smile and strut and leave them.

Auntie Eileen say I growing up now and I must learn to keep my legs closed. That Eileen must take me for a fool. Her school teacher boyfriend have a wife (I hear her on the phone quarreling with him), but I bet you that not stopping Eileen from swinging her legs wide open. I had a mind to give Auntie Eileen a piece of my mind, but then she would only slap me and say I too force-ripe. So I say, Auntie Eileen, I not even interested in boys, but she act like she don't even hear me.

Anyway, I too busy for Auntie Eileen and her foolishness; the other day I take home some of the periwinkle and plant them in the backyard because I practicing to be a florist from now. The yard already have a few croton and thing, so I off to a good start. But what this yard need is a tree—a big one. There's a little lime tree over in one corner but nothing more. Auntie Eileen promise to take me to country one week-end; maybe I'll find some flowers there.

Conversation on a Verandah:

. . . When it rain and stop and rain and stop like this, them call it "ole
woman rain" . . .
. . . And then them have some bird they call "ole woman bird"—these birds
swallow lizard, so sometimes they call them "lizard bird."

Five

DOWN THE ROAD there's a ole woman that always sit down on her
verandah. Every afternoon I pass and wave and she wave back to me. She
name Mrs. Cummings and the name well suit her because one day I stop
and ask her why she always sit down just looking like that and she tell
me say she waiting for the second coming. I say, Who coming? and she
say, The Lord. Anyway, me and Mrs. Cummings turn good friend. Her
daughter and her son-in-law always at work, and daytime just she alone
leave in the empty house, so sometimes I go over there and she tell me
all bout the flowers them in her yard—where they did come from and
how they get their name and how to grow them and and all kinda thing
like that. Mrs. Cummings give me a flowers name Ginger Lily. She say I
must take good care of it and it will bloom nice and big for me. When I
tell her how I going to country soon, she get all excited and she say I
must try see if I can find her some Madam Fate. I never hear about this
Madam Fate before but Mrs. Cummings tell me everything bout what it
look like. She say it going to have some star flowers on there, and she
say when I looking for it I mustn't call out its name or else I won't find
it. Mrs. Cummings say she well need the Madam Fate because she have
a ole ole pain and she going to soak Madam in some good strong white
rum and rub it on the pain.

• • •

So anyway, more news from Brooklyn! Muriel say she invite Andrea to dinner, and from the way Franklin carry on, she have a feeling he have the hots for Andrea. Muriel never tell me all this; she write and tell Auntie Eileen, but when Eileen gone to work I look in her draw and read Muriel letters. (Muriel business is my business, so I don't care.) Muriel say she sorry now say she did ever invite Andrea to eat with them, not that she find any fault with Andrea, but she say Franklin never been the type you can trust to think with his head.

So I say to Mrs. Cummings, Why they call the bush Madam Fate? And Mrs. Cummings laugh and say is because sometime when you in trouble the Madam is your last straw, and if you don't find her, you sure to keel over and just curl up and dead.

Six

So far my little garden doing well. I plant the periwinkle in a long row along the back fence but they already spread out all over the place just like they couldn't wait to come here and fill up the whole yard. At first I was worried that they wouldn't take to Eileen backyard, but they don't seem to mind at all; they laugh and talk to me same way, just like when I go over to the Garden. Mrs. Cummings look at my fingers and tell me say she can tell I have a way with flowers and that really really make me happy. Whole day I couldn't stop smile; even Eileen have to ask me is what I have up my sleeve that sweeting me like that.

That's the thing with Eileen, you know, she always wondering bout what I up to. If I push out my mouth, she say I too screw face, and if I smile and happy, she say I too trickify. She say she can already tell say I going to be one of those young girl that shoot out bosom quick-quick and develop and turn woman before you can even blink your eye, and that's why she have to keep an early watch on me because she know of dangers unseen. Last week she go and she buy me what she call a "training bra." I say, But Auntie, is what I have to train already? Auntie Eileen just toss it on the bed and say, Put it on. Cho, I not wearing the bra, it feel like a harness. I hope my breast them grow long and wagga-wagga just like Auntie Nora own . . . Imagine the look on Eileen face!

In my dream, the bones at the bottom of the sea smooth and white just like someone polish them up that way, the little fingers all sprawled and reaching; I wonder where all their skin gone to?

Maybe the fishes ate it all off, slowly bit by bit. Then maybe a fisherman did catch the fish and give to his wife and she fix it up nice and feed it to all her hungry pickney them, and the pickney them nyam and fill their bang-belly and lick their fingers and get up from the table and leave the pretty white bones stretch-out right there in the middle of the empty plates.

If you don't believe me, go ask the River Mumma; she live way up inna the source of all the river dem, and she know bout all these tings first han'. Wash your foot and go around middle-day, and if you keep quiet and look good, you will see her sit down pon one rock a dry her hair. Sometime you look and will see her a comb it, but long time she don't bother with that no more because her hair well bushy, and when water wet it, it too hard to comb. Don't let nobody fool you say she going grab and drown you. Is lie them a tell. When you go, bring a gift; find a nice speckle rockstone and blow on it three time. When you step in the water, make sure your two foot in there because you don't want River Mumma to tink say you have one foot a water and one foot a bank like you is a Thomas. When River Mumma see you, she going call you with her finger. When she call you, walk go to her; she only come out when river low anyway, so nothing not going happen to you.

When you reach, give her the rockstone, and she going take your head in her two han', and look if it have any junju or lice in there a scratch you, and then she going wash your hair in the river and she going soap it good with something smell like Sinkle Bible. Then after that now she going look for more junjo again and wash and rinse. She going wash three time, and after the third time now, she going clear her throat and say, Alright, so who send you?

Seven

AUNTIE EILEEN DON'T like go country no more; she is a town woman now, and she say every time she go country, mosquito and ticks bite her up, and she can't even take a good shower so it just not worth all the botheration. Anyway, she finally take me to country because she say she want to get Muriel off her back.

The road that go to Kings Pen have whole heap o' rock and pot hole, and the bus just a jigga-jigga and carry on, and the whole time Eileen just a kiss her teeth, cheups, cheups. Every time we turn a corner, I almost think the bus was going tip and turn over. A woman in the bus had a bag o' guava, and one time when the bus turn all the guava them spill out, and this cause heap o' confusion because who wasn't stepping on her guava was slipping them in their pocket or eating them. One of the guava slide in between my feet and I bend down and pick it up and put my head between my knees and bite it. The guava sweet to no end, but I never want Eileen see me eating the lady things, so I keep it hide in my pocket and every time she not looking I take a little bite.

Finally we reach Kings Pen and as soon as we get out the bus it start rain. Eileen never like that at all because rain mean mud, and mud mean that all her shoes and stockings going get spoil up. Anyway, Eileen put up her umbrella and we walk the mile and a half to go up to Miss Leela yard.

Auntie Eileen say Miss Leela dead long time but two of her grandson live in the yard now. The two grandson, Delbert and Albert, is Muriel and Eileen uncles, so that mean say them is my gran'uncle. Delbert and Albert is twins; they was living for a long time over in Panama, but now they come back to dead in them mother house. When we reach up by the yard, sun was coming down and the sky all orange like someone cray-on it up. Eileen put on her country voice and she call out, Uncle Del—oye! A ole man come to the door, a small-small man with a white goatee. He step out on the verandah and squint up two tamarind seed eye, and he say, Is who? No sooner he say that than another little ole man with the same white goatee peep out from over his shoulder.

Uncle Del and Uncle Al so glad to see us, you woulda think say is heaven we just come from. Uncle Del is the talky-talky one, and Uncle Al is the quiet one. Neither of them never married, and as far as them know neither of them have any pickney (although I did hear Eileen talk say a woman in Belize did have baby for one of them, and when she go to Uncle Del he say, Hell, no, is must be Al own, and when she go to Uncle Al he say, Uh-uh, is Del baby that).

Anyway, Uncle Del say the whole of we family either scatter-scatter or about to dead-off and is a shame but nobody don't hardly visit wi one another no more. He say the two of them spend time in Panama and Belize and Cuba, and now they come back to sit down on their Gran'mamsie verandah and keep company with the twelve ackee trees.

The first morning in Kings Pen, bright and early, I take out the map Muriel send me and I go walking around in the yard. It wasn't hard to find my Gran'mamsie coconut tree because is the only coconut tree in the yard and it tall and lean just like how Muriel draw it. Uncle Al say when him and Uncle Del were boys they used to climb this tree and they used to look out on the sea and wish say them did have a boat. (I wonder if is that Gran'mamsie did thinking bout, too.)

The twelve ackee trees stand up around the yard so comfortable, you would think them is people. I find a long stick lean against the side of the house and I go from one to the other looking for ackee to pick.

After I spot the way to Marse Percy yard, I quick time figure out which one is Miss Leela tree. This tree full up with ackee and I take the stick and reach and poke and reach and poke, but no matter how I try, not even as much as an ackee seed woulda fall down. This get me aggravate and my arm start to tired and my shoulder feel like it going to pop, so I look around and I find a box and I stand up on it and I reach and grab one of the ackee limb them and I shake it like all hell brucking loose, but still no ackee. All this time Uncle Del and Uncle Al sit down on the verandah watching me with a little smile on their face like two he-goat. Still Miss Leela hold on to her ackee and wouldn't give me none, and that's when I say to myself, Climb Gracie, climb, and I put my foot on a bump on Miss Leela bark and push myself up, and then I put the other foot on another bump and push again, and I stretch my arm and reach for a limb and next thing you know, Miss Leela stretch out one of her wrinkle arm and give to me and I hold on to her and she ease me up little higher, and I wrap my arms around her neck and she push me higher again till I start to feel good and I say to myself, Before I leave I *must* climb Gran'mamsie coconut tree.

Eileen say the water in country give her run-belly and she can't take it no more, so she going to go back to town. This alright with me because she say she going to let me stay for two more week with Uncle Del and Uncle Al. Uncle-them have a woman from over gully that come around twice a week to help wash and clean and see to it that everything alright. She name Althea and she tell me say she and my Mamsie was school mates. Me and Althea sit down on the back porch with my basket of ackee and we pull them from out the pods. She show me how to cut out the red string them, and then we wash the ackee clean-clean and Althea cook it up nice with saltfish and onion and thing.

    After we eat and done, I ask Althea what ackee good for and she say she don't know, but a long time ago white people was bringing plants and trees from Africa same like how them was bringing people.

Eight

EVERYDAY SINCE I HERE in country, I go out walking and looking for Madam Fate. Althea say I must mind how I walk because badness can jump out on you from out the bush same like how gunshot does bang and bruck loose in town. I say, Yes Miss Althie, I will mind how I walk (but as far as I concern, nothing can't worse than the dungle, so I not fraid at all).

Everyday I looking for Madam but I can't find her. So much flowers and leaf all bout the place that I get confuse. Maybe Madam don't grow around these parts no more, but poor ole Mrs. Cummings, how I could go back to town and let her down like that?

Althea tell me a story bout when she and Muriel was two school girl. She say one time they went to river to play and they were washing their dolly babies in the river when all of a sudden they see a woman yellow panties coming down in the river water. Althea say they look around but they never see anybody bathing or washing clothes or anything like that, so they take out the panties and put them to one side.

A few days past, and Althea say they go back to the same spot because they like that spot, and the two of them was splashing up in the water when all of a sudden they see a pair of stockings coming down in the river water. The pair of stockings long-long like whoever wear them must be a real langie-la-la. Althea say they look around but they never see anybody there, so they take the stockings and spread them out on a rock to one side.

Althea say a few days pass again and this time they was catching crayfish, and when they look they see a pretty-pretty head-scarf coming down the river. The head-scarf so nice that they had to reach out and take it quick before water carry it away, and they put it to one side to dry.

This thing go on and go on—every time they go river, they go to the same spot and they always find something different swimming down the river like it lost its owner—sometimes is a wash cloth, sometimes is a brassiere, all kinda thing like that, and every time they find it, they don't see who it come from, so they put it to one side, and then when they go back few days later somebody, only-God-knows-who, already take the things and gone.

Althea say this thing go on for a whole summer holiday till one day they were playing and they see a hair comb coming fast-fast down the river. Muriel reach out and grab the comb—one of those nice wide-tooth plastic hair comb, and she quick time put it in her pocket and take it home. Althea say from that day on when they go to river nothing more never come.

So I say, Althea, is where the comb now? Althea say, Muriel lost it.

Nine

BUT ANYWAY, I WAS telling you about Madam Fate. Only one more week left for me to go back to town, and I still can't find her. The other day while Uncle Del and Uncle Al inside snoozing, I go on out walking in the bush to see if I see any flowers look like her. I find ceracee and I find mint just like how Muriel write and tell me, and I find leaf-of-life because Mrs. Cummings have that one growing under her window, and she say if wasn't for that, pressure woulda done kill her long time. I see whole heap o' dandelion and Spanish needle, and of course, I see periwinkle (Althea say if is an egg, you can be sure periwinkle will be right there in the red).

I pick and smell and pick and smell, this and that flowers and this and that leaf, and I walk and walk till I start wonder if I shoulda turn back. By this time I reach a place have heap o' mango, black mango and common mango and stringy mango, all kinda mango just sweeting up the air, and I start to pick them up and eat them and I shove some in my pocket and some in my string-bag, and when I couldn't find any more space, I stuff two of the small ones in my training bra, and that's when a mongoose cross right in front of me and I hear like a broom brushing all busy and quick-like. I step little ways from out the mango-walk to look, and I see a ole bruck-down shacka-shacka house and I see a woman sweeping up leaves from off the front steps.

The woman brush the dry leaf them into a big ole pile and then she put sticks all around, and then she put more leaf and then she put more sticks, and I never know say the woman did even know say I watching her, but all of a sudden she turn around, and me and her eyes make four and she say, You have anything need burn?

The woman house have whole heap o' carve-up calabash, and thing prettying the verandah. Some of them hanging from the ceiling and have fancy flowers growing from outta them, and some of them fix onto the wall and have some funny picture cut into them. I see one that look like it have two ground lizard kissing one another, and I see another one that have a lizard with a tail long and twirly all around and around, and if you try to follow the tail, you lose it and you have to start over. Calabash on the floor, calabash on the windowsill, calabash hang over the door, calabash even hang around the woman neck.

The woman say to me, You is whose pickney? Don't I know your face from somewhere? And I say, Me is the Bert-them gran'niece, Ma'm, and she smile and say, Ahh.

The woman yard have a big poinciana tree, and me and she sit down underneath there and watch the fire burn. She wasn't saying anything and I wasn't saying anything, neither, but it seem like that never mat-ter and anyway I did tired.

After a while she throw a stick in the fire and she clear her throat.

One time there was a woman name Auntie Moonie who was a riggler; she use to go aroun mekking rig-gles, and if anybody guess the riggle, them win someting, but if them don't guess it, then is them that woulda have to give her someting.

One Chrismus everybody sit down pon verandah and Auntie Moonie drink plenty-plenty rum and she feeling good so she jump up and she say, Alright now, everybody, riggle me this, riggle me that, guess me this riggle and perhaps not: Anancy have a pretty pretty daughter with a head full o' hair, and every time breeze blow, the hair ketch fire. Is wah? Auntie Moonie feeling so good that she say anybody guess the riggle, she goin let them pick as much breadfruit off her tree as can full up a basket.

Miss Connie was there and she say, I bet you I know is wah, and if I not right, I goin give you this ole cock wah Marse George jus give mi for Chrismus. Auntie Moonie say, Alright, and Miss Connie say, Is red ants! Is red ants the answer! Auntie Moonie shake her head, and she say, Hand over the cock.

Then Marse George, him get all vex with Miss Connie, and him say, Is how you coulda just bet off the tings wah mi give you like that? And him call out, Auntie Moonie, I goin guess you the riggle; if I lose, I goin give you this brand-new cutlass, and if I win, I want the basket o' breadfruit plus I want back the cock. Auntie Moonie say, Alright, and Marse George say, Pepper! Is pepper the answer! Auntie Moonie shake her head, and she say, hand over the cutlass.

Mrs. Hendricks was there (you know the one that just come back from Henglan' and go on like she can't talk fe we talk no more). Hear her, Oh, Auntie Moonie, I have a really nice pot and I think I know the answer. Auntie Moonie say, Alright, and Mrs. Hendricks say, Oh, it's a strawberry cream pie! Oh, isn't it, Auntie Moonie! Auntie Moonie shake her head and say, Hand over the pot.

By this time Auntie Moonie start smack her lips because tings working out better than she did even tink: She have a cock, she have a cutlass, and she have a pot. Heh. Tings go on and on till only one woman, Mabel, don't mek a guess yet. She sit there listening everybody, and she say to herself, I mus can figure this riggle. Now Mabel did have a house full o' hungry pickney, so she wasn't playing the riggle for sport and she neva want tek no fool chance. Long time now Mabel did have to be tunin her han' with little this and little that trying to put food inna the pickney them belly because she was a one-mind woman and she wasn't goin just sit down and watch her children dead. Sometime all she have is a han'ful o' peas, but she add little water and she add little salt and she add little thyme, and while pot on fire, she might go outside and look if the tomato them bearing or somebody might stop by and give her an onion or couple chocho, and next thing you know, she find piece o' this and she add piece o' that and she work her brain and make a one-pot sweeter than yu woulda ever believe. Anyway, still, tings get tough so till Chrismus come,

and the only ting Mabel coulda find inna her cupboard was a box o' matches.

Mabel sit down watching Auntie Moonie—by this time the
verandah full up with all kinda mango and ackee and coconut and ting—
and Mabel say to herself, This box o' matches can't do me no damn good
if I don't have nothing to boil over it, so if I answer the riggle and lose, I
won't be no more worse off than before, but if I win, then me and the pickney them will lick we finger for weeks.

Mabel consider the riggle and she consider
the riggle and she take out her matches box and she say, Auntie Moonie, I
goin guess you the riggle, but if I lose, the only thing I can give you is this
matches box. Auntie Moonie look at the little ole matches box, and then she
look at Mabel in her hang-pon-nail ginger-bag frock, and she tink to herself,
Is wah this pitchy-patchy can pull on me anyway? So she say, Alright.

By this time the woman had my two ears growing longer and longer
and I look at her, all ready to hear is how the story going done. But she
just laugh to herself and she throw another stick in the fire and she
turn and look at me and say, Is your story now—finish it any way you
want.

Ten

THE NIGHT BEFORE I leave Kings Pen, I go outside while everybody sleeping and I climb Gran'mamsie coconut tree. I start and I fall and I start and I fall, but then I find out how it work and Gran'mamsie ease me up higher and higher in the moonshine. In the dark, the sea so pretty and smooth and bright, you woulda never believe so many little bones lay down all stretched out underneath it.

So I there hugging the tree with all fours, and I want to reach out and pick one of the coconut them, but my arms getting weaker and I fraid I might fall and I think bout the Bert-them finding my bones all crushed at the bottom of Gran'mamsie tree in the morning, and that's when I remember how I have to go home next day without finding Madam, and I feel all sick to my stomach like I have a ole ole pain, and I quick time make my way down.

Mrs. Cummings

Woman Dying on a Hospital Bed

For hours the shadows move
    in and out
of the room,
pausing by the doorway,
    hovering above,
blocking your view.

The ceiling—wide and smooth like fresh calico—calms you,
and you stitch on it all day
requilting your Eight-Pointed Star—
the one you pieced from bright scraps (saffron and amber),
for eighty years
and eight children.
Now the shadows surround your bed,
hushed and still like the moment between each Word of God.
This has been a long project—
you've liked your stitches small and straight.
Your fingers shaky,
you take your time,

thread in thread out

stitch	by stitch	by stitch	by
stitch	by stitch	by stitch	by
stitch	by		

(You must rise up on your elbow,
holler for one of the children
to come in from the yard, and thread your needle

    with

    strong

    black

    thread

    strong

    black

    thread

    for

    the eye)

Tonight,
only you see the needle disappear from the calico—
a thin swift light like a falling star.

One

I'M GOING TO SIT RIGHT here on the front verandah and wait for the Resurrection. From my old rocker, I have a good view of the cemetery across the street, the tombstones them dotting the top of the hill like pot lids waiting to pop off. See that fancy gray one over there, under the tamarind tree? That's Mary Atkins'. We used to go to school together, you know. Both of us grew up right here in town. We did play and jump rope right in the middle of this same-same street. Those were the days before all the traffic passing through; people here had mules. My Daddy used to have an old one-ear mule, Vickie (named after Queen Victoria). One time me and Mary was riding Vickie, sneaking out of church early, and she throw us right into that hibiscus bush. Me and Mary, Lord, I tell you, we did so much together, married two brothers you know—Patrick and Percy . . .

Ahh, look at that white dove perched right on Mama's grave! Did you know that if Mama was alive today, she would be one hundred and fifteen years old? *One hundred and fifteen.* I was born when Mama was thirty, the same age as me when I had my first girl, Sherline. Not only that, but she got married at thirty-one, and *I* got married at thirty-one. Now I'm the same age Mama was when she died! And listen, I am a woman with good sense (I used to be a school teacher, you know), and this means only two things to me: Either I am about to die, too, or some big change about to take place. Sherline say the births and marriages were just coincidence, but between me and you, I don't believe in coincidence, and since I don't feel ole Marse Death knocking on my bones right now, that leave only one thing.

So I start to think, you know, just thinking. Then one evening I was out here on the verandah, drinking my ceracee tea, taking my medicine, and God be my judge, I'm not lying, with my two eyes wide open, a vision unscroll itself in front of me—light pouring down over everything—the whole hill lit up; all the mangoes on the trees, gold, and the oranges, silver. Mama step from behind that poinciana tree in the corner, wearing the same blue plaid dress we bury her in, but her skin smooth and new. Then I see Mary and ole Mr. Sanders (he used to sell us roast peanuts when I was a child) and Auntie Enid (she had sugar and they had to cut off her two feet) and then—in a circle of the whitest light—Percy, young and with a full head of hair, singing the song Mama sang at our wedding, O Love Divine. Percy come to the curb, right where you see that car parked there now, and a voice say, "Not yet." Soft, just like that, "Not yet," and same time, the vision disappear and all I could see was the tombstones them standing up all still on the hill.

Now I tell Sherline about the vision. I say is a vision of the second coming, the Resurrection. Sherline say is my medicine. Errol, her husband, agree with her. I never did like Errol, always scorning at Truth. He teach chemistry at the High School and don't believe in anything he can't see, hear, or smell. Evenings now, I keep to myself and just watch and hum. When it really happen, I think it going be at night, light breaking through the darkness, O love divine . . . but I don't even point out Percy grave to you yet! His is the one that lean a little to the right. Over there. See? The one with the low fence around it. The Conroys' goat had a way of eating at the crotons I plant for Percy, and leaving little droppings all over the tombstone them, so I dip into my savings and had a little wire fence made. There's a gate with a latch, and when my arthritis not too bad, I go there to just speak my mind and think.

Two

LONG TIME I BEEN wanting to tell you bout Gracie—a little chile from down the road that turn my good-good friend—such a bright little thing and no bigger than a matches stick. Sherline and Errol send away the grandchildren for summer holiday, so if it wasn't for Gracie, I don't know what I would do all day, locked up here in this empty house like I in jail. When Gracie come over, my ole pain them don't bother me so bad, the two of us do little weeding or little watering, and I tell you, I don't know what it is about that chile, but God be my judge, sometime she look at me like she is older than her years—like she done understand all bout life already. When she look at me like that (now this is just between me and you), I almost want to pour out my heart and tell her bout how that Percy did beat me in front of my owna children and how this vexation well up inside me for thirty years like rotten jack-fruit. I almost want tell her bout how I can't wait to see him in the next life so I can trace him out and kick him straight through to hell (somehow I believe she would understand), but then I catch myself and I keep my mouth shut because how can I break down now and bawl on the shoulder of a young pickney-chile who not even wearing brassiere yet? Lord, if I did only have some Madam Fate.

• • •

So don't get to thinking that everybody you see up on that hill going to
be caught up to meet the Lord in the air. Take that tag-rag Gayle
Simons, for instance. See her there—the headstone right at the road-
side where she can nosy in people's business. Sometimes you walk by
her grave, and just a *bad* smell hangs in the air. The cement on her
tomb all cracked up . . . busy-body! even in death. Let me tell you something now (and don't you tell anybody this): Years it's been the talk
around here that Deacon Owen's first boy is not really his, and not a
truth in the rumor. But guess who started it? Gayle. She used to do
domestic work for the family, you know. Anyway, she had a run-in with
the wife, and decided to leave and kick up dust. I could tell you some
things about that woman. Mercy, Father, just looking at that old
cracked-up tomb gets my asthma and all the ole pain them started.

But don't go and forget that what my mouth slip and mention bout
Percy beating me is just between you and me and it not to leave from
outta this room. I too ole to be opening up Pandora's Box. Uh-uh.
When the Resurrection come I going greet him and give him a nice
smile and a holy kiss (while I have my foot set and waiting to kick). But
in the meantime, from here on when I speak bout Percy, I going put
that plan aside and say he was a *good* man—because in some ways he
really was. You understand? Okay.

Speaking of asthma, yesterday the doctor come to visit (I can't take the
driving, you see), a nice young doctor from the university in town. He
remind me a little of Percy when he was young, teeth white like
coconut fresh from the husk and a neat little black moustache. I tell
him bout the vision and he *listen*, the whole time looking into my eyes
all intense-like. He didn't say much bout it, but I could tell he understand. That Dr. Ramsey is a good young man, and I bet you he is a
Believer too. Afterward I watch Sherline and Errol pull him aside, whispering, trying to turn him against the Truth . . . but wait, did I tell you
about Mary Atkins? Hers is the fancy gray tomb under the tamarind

tree. We grew up together you know, right here in town. Used to jump rope right in the middle of this same-same street.

> *Mary,*
> *Mary,*
> *quite contrary,*
> *how does*
> *your garden*
> *grow?*

Three

GRACIE STOP BY TODAY, say she going to country. I going miss her, bless her heart, and I already can't wait until she comes back; plus guess what? Maybe she can find me some Madam Fate.

It's funny how time drags by when you're waiting for someting. If it weren't for Jane and Louisa, I don't know what I'd do. Jane and Louisa have pictures on my bedroom wall. They are English ladies and wear long flowery dresses with gloves and big wide hats. Louisa's the one that hang above the dressing table, sitting in her garden and drinking tea. Jane is the one with the parasol and sad eyes. Sometime they both sit on my bed and we exchange stories and have a good ole time. Jane's husband is a duke; he beats her, you know, that's how she lost her two children before they were even born, and that's why she always sad. Louisa's husband passed away some years ago. He was rich, left her heaps of money, and now she bored and just drink tea all day or talk to us. I tell them all about Percy. At my wedding I wore gloves just like Louisa's, white crochet. Mary Atkins was my matron-of-honor; by this time she was already married and pregnant with Leroy. Percy was such a good man, a *good* man, you know? When we were courting he used to live over in Broadbridge, and would walk ten and a half miles, *ten and a half miles*, to come see me. Anyway, as I was saying, Louisa have the most lovely voice. I teach her all the words to *O Love Divine* and she loves it. Jane, now, she do the most beautiful needle work. She hand-stitching me a new handkerchief for the Resurrection, you know, and I do believe they have both quite managed to give me an English accent. *O Love Divine.*

Yesterday Jane and Louisa had just left when (God be my judge) I turn around and see Mary standing in the bedroom doorway. She had her hair in white ribbons and was carrying that calico doll I give her. I say, "Mary!" but it was as if she couldn't hear me and I couldn't hear her. I see her lips moving, you know, but couldn't make out a word. Now what that could mean? She needs me, I know it! Jane understands. Her babies them come to her, secretly, in the lovely garden behind her house. Sometimes she see them laying back there all scratched up by the rose thorns but she can't move her feet; is as if she stuck to the ground and can't save them. Nobody know about this but Louisa and Jane and me. Jane and Louisa have lovely gardens, roses, roses every-where. At night the roses bloom, bloom higher and higher against my window and all along the door frame, pink and red and yellow, shutting out the noise of Errol's t.v., something about the smell reminding me of that song—maybe you've heard it. It's in those ole, ole-time hym-nals, and is called *O Love Divine.*

I am growing tired of waiting. My knees hurt, so do the joints of my fin-gers, and sometimes when I look over to the hill, my heart just goes flippity flap flap flap, over and over and faster and faster until I have to catch my breath and go take some medicine and lay down, but I must be strong. The Resurrection will be here anytime now, in a moment, in the twinkling of an eye, hallelujah.

Then that Errol confirmed what I knew all along: He want to get rid of me. I never did like Errol. He is a Hodge—one of those Hodges from LaGuardia that think much of themselves, standoffish. Believe me,

Errol don't like the Truth. He teach chemistry at the High School and fools around with chemicals in a corner of the kitchen, always mixing up this and mixing up that. To tell you the truth, I am glad that time is short because God be my judge, any day now, Errol is set to blow this whole blasted place up.

Now, don't go spreading this around, but last night I heard Sherline and Errol talking in the living room. Errol said (referring to me), "We might have to send her away." Sherline just walked over to the window, didn't even put up a fight for me or anything. I see her carry on like that time and time again. She was always like that anyway, easily influenced. I always knew I couldn't depend on her in my ole age. Then Errol say, "She talking to them picture on her wall now," and then listen to this part: "Rass, Sherline, the kids them fraid of her, she think Gracie, that girl from down the road, is Mary what-her-name!" Can you believe this man? Plotting to turn my own flesh and blood against me. Now I am a woman with good sense (I used to be a school teacher, you know), so what would I be doing talking to a picture on my wall? Two ole-time white ladies in fancy clothes and English gardens and me an ole woman from back o' water! Nonsense. And why would I scare my own grand-children? Mary is dead. Look through the window, see her tombstone over there, under the tamarind tree. God be my judge, *of course*, I know Gracie is not Mary. If only Percy were here. He had a way of setting things straight. He died of lung cancer, you know. A good man, and a hard worker. Even when we were young, and everyone else around did-n't have two sticks to rub together, Percy kept food on the table, clothes on our backs, a roof over our head. I remember our wedding day. Percy, handsome in his dark suit. I wore the same white dress my mother wore. My hair was thick then, and black. Percy had given me a pretty little wrist watch, and I wore white crochet gloves, just like Louisa's.

Woke up this morning but still no Gracie and no Madam Fate. Sherline came in to tell me Dr. Ramsey coming later on, and (you won't believe this) she ask how would I like to live in a nursing home where I can get more help. A home! I was right, they want to get rid of me. Today she says is a "home," but next thing you know, Jesus help me, it will turn out to be the Garden. Percy and me built this house with our own hard-earn money, and now they want to throw me out of it. They going put me in a nursing home with green walls and all that smelly food. Next week, she say, next week! I not going, I not going, I say. Is the doctor idea, not mine, she say. Ah hah! So they finally turn Dr. Ramsey against the Truth! If I don't hurry get little Madam Fate, only the Resurrection can save me now. Here I am an ole woman, sitting on my own verandah watching the cemetery I live across from all my life, and now I'm to be taken away to some home, just like that. This is the street I live my life on, me and Mary jumped rope right in the middle of this same-same street. I used to ride my Daddy mule here, and tie it to that poinciana tree by the corner. Mama did live here, too; she die in this same house. That's her grave, the white one in the middle. What's an ole woman like me to do, my heart going flippity flap flap, when plans already been made to put me away? Listen: flippity flap, flap flippity flap flap. I remember when I was pregnant with Sherline, Percy used to listen for her heart through my belly. He was such a good man; that's his grave there with the low fence around it. These are his eye's glasses here in my pocket; he didn't want to be buried with them. His mother, now, she was buried with her gold-rim glasses, a full set of dentures, and a new gray wig. She died in her own home with her sons and daughters around her bed. I always knew Errol was a scamp. A nursing home! Can you believe it? But listen to my heart. Listen to it again: flippity flap flap, flippity flap flap . . .

Ahh, there come Dr. Ramsey car now. He in on this. They've turn him against me, or was he on their side all along? Funny, how people can just pick up and change on you from one day to the next. There he is getting out, wearing his little white jacket. I must get up from this chair, find my slippers, get away to the bedroom. Isn't this the same bad breeze I did feel the night Mr. Marshall sacrifice all ten fingers from the hands of his daughters, saying it was time they stop pointing at him every time things went wrong? The little one, Sheila, bled to death; that's her grave right over there—

But here comes the white jacket and I *must* get up. Look at the stethoscope swinging from his hand like a two-head snake. Listen to how he slam the car door; this is not a friendly visit at all. How I didn't noticed how big and cuuba-cuuba his feet was before? Look at how he kick the gate open with his foot, nuh, walking across the grass, crush-ing my periwinkles.

Jesus, where Gracie with the Madam Fate?

And those corduroy pants—everyone know you don't wear corduroy in this heat. Look at the leather on his bag, all crack-up and ashy like dry skin, and this one much larger than the one he did have before; he must be hiding something, but what it could be? Look at his hands his hands his . . . Oh, but, Percy, is you! You are here. I knew you would come. You look so handsome with your hair all trimmed. Yes, let me fix your tie, but don't you know it's bad luck to see the bride right before the wedding? Here, look at my gloves, I made them myself, and the wrist watch you gave me, see? But don't lift my veil yet, already my eyes full with water—you know how I get when I'm happy. Percy, take my hands and squeeze them, squeeze them; soon we going to wear little circles like light around our fingers. You and me. Listen, Deacon Grant playing the organ, and look at the periwinkle bobbing from side to side, growing brighter and brighter. Such a deep purple! They know. They know. Look at them climbing higher and higher, their face them shape just like live hearts against the wall. Put my kerchief in your pocket for a bit of luck, Percy, and take my arm. Take my arm. This our day, yours and mine. Oh Love love love. Divine. Divine.

Ida

STRAYED or STOLEN
From the Parifh of St. Andrew,
June 15, 1788
A BLACK MULE
with brown and white fpeckles on both ears
and a flight limp.
Anyone perfon finding faid mule pleafe report to
MR. FREDERICK DILLINGS.
Fuch perfon fhall receive a fmall reward.

One

PEOPLE ASK WHY I LEAN and walk with a limp. Somehow from my eyes was at my knee, I always feel lopside. But you know what, I spend couple years in the Garden and I watch Nurse Watson with her hoity-toity talk, don't know east from west, head from tail, snake from grasshopper, and I get to understand things different: Is not me that lopside, is *the world* that lopside, so it look to everybody like I leaning all out the way, when I only trying to get my bearings and keep my two foot on the ground. That's how I see it. Mama, now, she would say, when the Lord come he going set all crooked things straight.

But, anyway, now that I bring up Mama, I might as well let you know I have a bone to pick with her. Years she dead now and she don't make not even a squeak to me from out the calabash. Papa, now, he was always the quiet one that don't say much, so I wasn't expecting to hear from him, but Mama—good Lord she could at least say howdy-do. As much as I bawl at her funeral, Mama Mama Mama, even lose my voice, you woulda think she would put pride aside and talk to me. But no, she did so convince herself she don't believe in duppie and duppie bad for me and duppie going get me in trouble that now she herself turn duppy and she don't want admit to it. Anyway, Mama, one day I going dead and cross to your side, and me and you will have a talk. And don't try tell me how you is somewhere drinking milk and honey with the Lord neither because I tell you what: I see God over by Marse Howard banana and she did running around barefoot, poorer than two of us put together.

But anyway, chile, come over here to the verandah and let me show you the calabash them. I leave Kings Pen and spend time over in the Garden and come back and find the house just like how I did leave it, not even a thread outta place. People have all kinda story bout me, you know, they believe I can set goozuum on them, and because of that even tief stay away—good for me. Look, not a thing did get touch, not even by Hurricane Gilbert. But wait, I forget my manners! You want a cup of tea? Hold on there, let me put pot on fire and boil a little ceracee.

So, as I was saying, the house full up with even more calabash now than ever before. I use to carve one and then I get another idea or I hear another voice and carve up a next one, and before I coulda say, Jack Mandora, the whole place start fill. Now this one that you see here, one half in my basket and one half in my brassiere, well, is the same-same one that the iron-collar boy did give me. (And since I mention it, let me go ahead and tell you bout how it is I only have one breast. Well, one time a woman talk to me from outta the calabash. This woman was from before your time and mine, Guinea she come from, you know, but she did have a ole ole pain stick like poison arrow in her breast, and she did want see if I coulda listen her story so it could get balm. I say, Alright, and she say all I have to do is grate little arrow root, and when night come I must go out by the beach and sprinkle it and let the sea carry it away. I do what she tell me, I get the arrow root and I walk along the seaside and drop little here and drop little there as I go along, the whole time the calabash to my ears. I walk the full length of the beach till I come to a bend, and that's when I hear a splashing like water knocking up against the side of a ship. I look around and I don't see anything, so I listen again and get to realize say is the calabash the sound coming from. Whoosh whoosh. I listen good and hear plenty voice on the ship, drumming and laughing, and I don't know why, but I never like the sound of that laughing at all and I start feel fraid. I listen and listen and I pick up another sound in the calabash, something like feet dancing on the deck, but the dance not sweet, no spirit in the dance, and I say to myself, this is a force dance. I hear more laughing. Wicked laughing, you know. Something tell me the laugh make for me and I start feel mad and I start feel shame. I smell the sea, and I realize say is a deep-deep sea this. I smell beer. I smell sweat. I feel something like a collar around my neck. I hear a whip one two three and I feel myself dancing the dance, trying to find the step, my feet dragging; I feel weak but I know I can't stop, I have to put out my best and do just like how they want me to do, they want to see my breasts them jump, they want me to stamp my foot and turn around and shake so they can watch me from behind. One two three. Dance dance dance. No no no. Look my baby over in the corner, poor little thing crying her head off. All this nasty laughing. And the ship heading straight for that line over there, we going all fall right over the edge. Off the edge of the world. Dance dance dance. Is my last dance this, my last chance, my war dance. Shake it, shake it. One two three. Look my baby over in the corner, poor little thing, coughing her head off. Shake it like this. Watch me jump/ and grab her/ and turn/ and swing her/ over the side/ into the water. It can't be any worse in there.

After that, the calabash get quiet, the sea spread out in front of me all shiny and smooth just like nothing never happen. I feel a pain shoot through my breast, and when I look down, the breast already wither and gone.)

Shake it like that.

Two

IN THE GARDEN they have a thing they call electric shock. This shock is a terrible thing because it make all the women them lose them remembrance. I tell you, I wouldn't wish this shock on my worse enemy (and I have some bad ones). They shock you up few times, and next thing, you walking around like a lock without a key. Is Claudia get me out of there, you know. Yes, is me and Mrs. Johnskin she did want help get out, but Mrs. Johnskin come down sick the day before and dead right there in Ward Three. I did hear it cause big fuss when I disappear, but Claudia say she go back there the following week and nobody don't even suspect her. She say the two bed me and Mrs. Johnskin sleep inna never even turn cold before they find next woman drop put in there.

Even if she did get out, poor Mrs. Johnskin woulda never even have a home to go back to; two of her children in jail and the only one that did amount to anything live over in Canada, wouldn't even write. Generation of vipers. Mrs. Johnskin did sickly you know, and the Garden just run her down even more. I wake up the morning and see her curl up in bed, almost stiff as a tree. I watch the nurse them quick time stretch her out and put her two arm to her side and fix her leg them long ways and I say to myself, Them shoulda just leave the dear soul curl up like a baby same way. Mrs. Johnskin never use to sleep comfortable on her back before, so why force her now? I tell you, if it was left to me, them woulda have two kinda coffin in this world, some round and some long, that way who like to curl up could curl up as much as them want and who like to lie down flat or on them side coulda do just that.

The good thing is, Mrs. Johnskin speak to me from out the calabash and she open out her heart to me better than even when we was in the Garden. Poor soul, her body still there freeze up in the hospital morgue because them can't contact nobody to come claim her yet. Mrs. Johnskin say is her fault because she never do enough for her children when them was growing up, and one of them she even take green pineapple and try dash away and another one she not even sure is who the father. I say, Johnskin, hush you mouth! I know mother love when I see it, and any how you look at it, these children you worrying over is a wuckless no-good generation.

So this is the calabash I working on now. I going call it "carry on" and I going give it to Claudia. All of them have a name, you know; that one over there with the spider plant growing out of it name "feather tongue," and this little one on the step name "river bottom." This one here I call "spit it out," that's for Bella—the best advice is always simple.

Three

I WORRY ABOUT CLAUDIA these days, she making this mother business take over her life. Still, I understand her concern to find her Mams, after all, even a ole woman need her mother. From the day she turn up at the Garden I know Claudia did searching for something. You can always know a woman when she that way, she have a look in her two eye like a pit without a bottom. You look in the pit and you feel how much she hungry. This hungry fill her up so till sometime her belly even start bloat.

Now that Claudia hear bout Johnskin, she getting all kinda idea bout how she need to go check out a few morgue. How she think she going to do that anyway, volunteer work? Claudia come in to me like all my three daughter wrap up inna one, and sometime when I see the scream in her two eye, I just want to hold her and say, is me, Is me you Ma now.

I'll never forget the afternoon we left the Garden. All morning me and Madda Wilma try call rain (to keep the nurse them nose inside) but not a cloud was in the sky. Later, Claudia come and take us to the crafts room, but still no rain. I sit down by the back door, dropping rice in my pan, but still no rain. The sky did have a bright bright blue that day, and if there's one thing you learn as a rainmaker, is that you can't trust the color blue, so you better outsmarts it. Heh, I take out my blue kerchief from out my brassiere, and I rub it and rub it and rub it between my two hands, playing like I washing it. The kerchief dry, but I wring it around and around like I squeezing out water. Then I rub some more and squeeze; and I rub some more and squeeze. I rub and I squeeze, I rub and I squeeze till the ole wrist them get sore, but I wring and wring and wring and wring till (ask Claudia, she will tell you) water start to squeeze out the dry kerchief—enough to fill the whole calabash. One of the women them was watching me, and she see it, and she say, Lawd Jesus-rass-a-mighty! Everybody turn round to look, and that's when sky bruck loose like all the waters in hell.

After crafts finish at three, *As the World Turns* did just getting started, and me and Claudia dash through the rain to the Rabbit. Ole Mr. Cameron was at the gate. I cover my head and keep it down, and Claudia speed on pass him. Claudia say Cameron did look half-sleep but then she say a funny thing happen. She look through her rear mirror and see him hoist up himself on his one foot watching the car drive off down the street. Claudia say she would bet any money, he was smiling.

I glad to be out of that slave pen, but I miss the periwinkle and I miss all my friends them. At one time they did have a woman in the Garden, Mimi, who all the while use to hear water in her head dropping, plop, into some deep-deep water hole behind her tongue. Sake of this everlasting dripping she couldn't even hardly talk. All day she listening to the water, counting to herself, plop two three four, till she must be did count over a million drops. I try everything to help Mimi, I sing for her, I dance for her, but nothing woulda stop the water, and that's when I get the idea to try rain. Something about rain can soothe you. Is water, but is pipper pipper pip, not plop plop plop. So I say to myself maybe she woulda like the story them that the rain carry and it might balm her.

So anyway, one day I talk to Madda Wilma and she help me call rain all soft and nice just like how I like it. It take us all morning, dropping rice in my rain pan, but by middle-day it come. I did there sitting under the ackee tree and Mimi leaning in the doorway; I did have the calabash to my ear, and after a while the rain so sweet, I almost forget why we call it. I believe I did just about to doze when a voice say, Ida! I know right away the voice was Mimi own, but it get me all puzzle because the voice coming from out the calabash while Mimi still over there leaning in the doorway, her two eye them watching the ground. Mimi voice come again, Ida! but she stand up same place in the doorway, rubbing one foot gainst the next one, not even paying me any mind. If she wasn't dead, is how she did calling from out the calabash like that? Plop plop plop. Chile, I hear that sound and my heart jump, baps! And that's when it come to me say all along this Mimi is really a duppie.

Rainy season again.

I find out say Mimi did dead few years before, curl up in the cabinet under her Mamsie kitchen sink. She did dose over with drugs, the leak under the sink making plop plop plop. After she dead, she come to the Garden so I could listen her story and balm her.

That night, rain pour down in the Garden five hours straight; when the nurse them make their rounds in the morning, Mimi gone.

Four

So ANYWAY, I SAY ALL this to say that you can't always just go by what you see in front of you with your two eye. Sometimes you looking low when you should look high. Sometimes you looking outside when you should look underneath. Take Bella, for instance, perhaps if I did know her true-true self, it would hard to believe all the brimstone and fire that she carry on with at night. Last week she talk to me from out the calabash, Ida! Ida! It was late night and I stand up by the window with the calabash to my ears, and that's when I see her in the distance—her hair on fire, running like mad through the mango walk. Oh God, I could hardly bear it. My face get hot, I feel my two eyes well up with water, and from deep inna my womb, a voice cry, Mamie! Such a scared little voice! The lizard them hear it, too, and start to bawl, still the kin-owl just keep running, red coals jiggling in her womb. I call out, Bella! and just as I say that, the fire disappear and the calabash turn quiet. My God, what to do with this kin-owl?

But listen, I have big news. One thing about the restless dead is that they love to run their mouth. Because of that, yesterday fresh story slip and come to me. And guess who Claudia mother is? Make a guess.

This calls for another cup of tea.

Muriel

Excerpt #54 from *Bush Bath for Tired Feet*

Gather your bush (try **Sinkle Bible, Rosemary, Lemon Grass, Tuna Cactus, Basil, Cucumber**) and pound it with a mortar and pestle. Tie the crushed leaves into an old stocking. Heat some rain water and pour into a small wash bowl. Allow the stocking bag to soak in the water alongside your feet. Invite a trusted friend(s). Light a red candle. Tell a story. (See also: **Purity Bath, Bush Tea, Poultice, Ole Woman Rain, Oil-of-mek-yu-walk, Oil-of-carry-on.**)

One

THE OTHER DAY I WAS on the A train going home when a woman get on begging for money. Hear her; Hello, my name is Yvette, I'm twenty years old, I'm homeless, and I'm HIV positive. Everybody play like them don't hear her, them keep them two eye in them newspaper or watch them reflection in the window glass. Something in the voice sound like a yardie, and when I look good, nuh, Mrs. Benjamin from over August Town wash-belly last daughter. Every time you see Mrs. Benjamin and ask her how the children, she always smile like full moon and go on bout how Yvette live in New York turn big-time model. Now listen to me, I know Mrs. Benjamin to be an honest woman (rosemary grow in her garden, and them say is only in the garden of the righteous that rosemary can thrive), so I know say she not trying to fool nobody. I bet you Yvette feel shame to break her mother heart, so she write and send letter to Jamaica full with lie, longer than eye-water. Yvette catch my eye and she quick time get off at the next stop because I bet you she did recognize me. I remember when Yvette was a nice pretty girl going to High School, she coulda been a model, for true, but look at her now, mash up like rotten breadfruit.

Gracie, the toilets going from bad to worse, but the weather turn like summer now and this give me joy. Sometime me and Andrea take Earlie and we go walking in the park. Abroad-people funny, you know, Gracie, you should see all of them jogging in the park around and around. Nothing wrong with that but some of them jog with them dog, some of them with them puss in them arm or them baby in stroller; I even see a man with a bird on his shoulder and all of them listening to a radio in them ears. Is like everybody turn mad and they don't care where they running to or what they running from, they just have a mind to run.

Andrea is a nice lady; you would like her. She say me and she use to go to the same school together when we were growing up but somehow I don't remember. Something about the way she look at me afterward make me think her tongue did slip and she say something she wasn't supposed to mention. It's funny, this New York big, but still, you never know who you can bump into that you did know from Timbuktu, and all of them seem to have a secret. Anyway, Andrea is a good friend to me, and if I'm in trouble and it's the last dollar she have, I know say she would help me and I would do the same for her, so it don't matter to me if she have one or two secret. So do I.

Monday morning I see Yvette again, this time standing up outside the Port Authority on Forty-second Street. Hello, my name is Yvette, I'm twenty years old, I'm homeless, and I'm HIV positive. Right then and there I decide in myself I must say something to this chile. Mrs. Benjamin wouldn't want me to come all the way to America and see her daughter destitute and just turn my back on her. So I walk up behind her and I whisper, Yvette? Yvette turn around, her two eyes them hollow like a pot without a bottom, and when she realize who calling her name, she tear off running across the street, car nearly lick her down.

Next time I see Yvette, I going say, Darling, come; don't worry, your secret is safe. Rosemary growing in your Mamsie garden.

Two

GRACIE, I'M STANDING by the kitchen window watching the night sky; you don't see much stars over Brooklyn, but I can see few tonight. That bright one over there must be the north star. Maybe you in Jamaica right now, watching the same star at the same time as me—at least that's what I woulda like to think.

One time (long before your time and mine), there was a woman in a thick thick forest running for her life. The overseer and his dog them was chasing after her. It was night and she couldn't see much but she could hear the dog them barking barking barking, bloodhounds, after blood. The woman did trying to reach a secret place inna the hills where her friends already leave and reach the week before and where she know she woulda be safe. The dogs them was getting closer and closer and the woman getting tireder and tireder till she almost ready to drop down, and she say to herself, Oh God, oh God, wah fe do?

This woman was a sensible woman, and she did know say if she keep going, the dog them woulda catch her and tear her up and Massa woulda beat her till she tell him where the rest o' them hiding. Maybe she coulda turn east and run to the sea—the sea woulda be happy to swallow her up and hide her, and that way Massa wouldn't get no chance to cross-question her—but the sea did too far that night, and she was so tired so tired so tired . . . So wah fe do?

The woman foot them was dragging and stumbling, her head start spin and she feel herself falling falling falling and she reach out and grab onto a tree. The dog them was nearer now, she could hear the man them shouting, and it sound to her like a thousand horse hoof pounding the ground. The woman gather all her strength together and hold on to the tree trying to ease herself up because she make up her mind say, if she have to get catch, she was going get catch running, not laying down. She lean gainst the tree, pushing herself up, and that's when she see a little lizard on the tree bark. Nothing wasn't strange bout that, but the little lizard have a shine-eye, and the shine-eye wink at her and the lizard whisper, "Shh, swallow me." At first the woman think say is must be "Follow me" the lizard say, but the lizard wasn't moving and she hear again, "Swallow me." By this time she could see the dog them moving through the trees. She look back quick at the lizard, it have the head tilt to one side, waiting. She hear someone shout, Wench! and she quick time grab the lizard and swallow it and

straightaway

she change into a bush with eight little flowers growing on there look just like stars. When the man and the dog them reach the tree them sniff around the bush and them look and them search, but them don't see no woman and everybody confuse.

Sometime when the night clear you can see the lizard up inna the sky, you know. Eight stars fix just like a zig zag because that's how the lizard like to walk, zig zag, zig zag, strutting her tail.

Ahh, quick, Gracie, make a wish . . .

Three

I STILL BUSY WITH my crochet work, and guess what? Andrea come up with an idea: She hear bout a crafts fair at a community center somewhere, and one weekend me and she and two other woman getting together to put up a stall. I doing all kinda thing now. I use pretty thread and I make some teeny-tiny crochet like hanging fruit and leaves and flowers, and I fix them onto hooks to make ears' ring. I going send you a special pair and I want you to tell me the honest truth whether you like them or not. Andrea think my ears' ring will go nice with her bead work. Then there's a friend of hers who makes clay pots, plus another friend who dries flowers.

I'm in the kitchen chopping onion. Franklin at work. Earlie sleeping. The periwinkle on the windowsill, listening. Your Auntie Eileen tell me how you sprouting up quick, and how you like to keep company with that woman down the road—what she name again? Mrs. Cummings. Mrs. Cummings is a nice woman, although her daughter and son-in-law don't worth two cents. Sometimes when I visit Eileen I used to call hello to her—she always sit down on her verandah—and it never fail that she have something from out her garden to offer me. She use to come trotting to the gate with a little mint or a bunch of crape myrtle or a nice Chinese hibiscus. Mrs. Cummings so proud of her garden, and she have a story to tell for every plant that in there. On top of that, she

the type of woman who will talk to death any-and everybody who will
listen so that sometime you just have to say, Sorry, Mrs. Cummings,
but I have to run. I never forget one time Mrs. Cummings did have a
duppie fly-trap flowers. She ever show you that one? Maybe not,
because it don't bloom all the time. The flowers big and pretty but it
stink like a rotten toe. She tell me you can learn plenty things from that
flower because the flower well trickify and then she go on to tell me
story bout which duppie she know that set trap for who and all kinda
horse dead and cow fat and the story did well sweet, but I start get vex
with myself because I end up listening to her for a full hour and I late
for work.

So Eileen say you sprouting up quick. I wish I could see you. Tell
your Auntie to make sure she take your picture and send come give me.
You eating up good? Night time before you go to bed, mix the powder
milk I send and drink it; add little honey or chocolate tea. Remember
to keep your head up, me and your father never raise you to be a come-
around Betty. After all these years, onion still make my eyes water.

Four

SO ANYWAY, I UP on thirtieth the other day when all of a sudden I just have a feeling that you in some kinda trouble. A bad cloud settle over me, real funny, and my heart start to beat all fast. I get so sick with worry that I had to sit down on one of the toilet them and rest my hand in my head. Girl, I hope everything alright. Long time you don't write to me. What happen? You still vex with me? I here working off my backside, sliding in people filth, and you there can't even pick up pen and paper to scratch, "Hello, cockroach." Jesus, do better than that, nuh! You think is streets of gold I walking on why I can't send for you? Eh? You think is fairy godmother them have in New York? Eh? You think is silver slippers I here sporting? Ungrateful no-good.

Anyway, hush. Sit next to me. You're a big girl now but not too big to sit by your Mamsie. Look this little flower I making. Come help me finish it. This stitch I doing name dB. Watch: (1) Thread around the needle, (2) needle into the crochet, (3) thread around the needle again, (4) then pull out—straight through two stitches—and is over! If you learn how the stitch them work, you can make any pattern you want, and not only that, you can make up your own pattern and call it what you like.

Row Three
1 bs in 1st ch., 4 ch., 6 B. in bs, 2 bs and 7 B.

(Repeat 2x)

In spite of what you think, I didn't swap Franklin for you. He's your father, after all, and he work hard to put food on the table. If you to come to 'Merica at all, it going to take the two of us to bring you over. I alone can't do it. And even with the two of us, sometimes is like we taking one step forward and two back. Sometimes me and him quarrel and I have a mind to leave the bastard, but then I think bout you. Is Franklin you look like you know, not me. I look at him and I see you— those eyes just like a chile.

Row Six
. . . 1 sk, 4B. 1 sk, 2 ch., 2 bs
(Repeat 2x)

I meet Franklin when I was a dancer at the Peacock Lounge. I bet you never know I coulda do them kinda dance, eh? I never like the work at all—worse than cleaning toilets—but bread have to go on the table somehow. Franklin come in and buy me two drinks after my shift, one night and that's how things did get start, simple as that. We go on and on—those days we did both lovey-dovey—till him say him woulda like married but him never want no wife dancing up in fronta heap o' man every night. Anyway, that's how I leave the Peacock, and two month later we go to the court house and tie the knot.

(Repeat as in the 5th & 6th row, increasing the number of petals until the flower attains desired dimensions.)

Sometimes me and Franklin quarrel and I have a mind to leave the bastard, but then I think bout you. I think bout you and I see your future spread like a table cloth, and even though I burn inside, I suck it all in.

Speak of the devil, and he sure to come, I better put down my sewings and go put rice on fire . . .

I

Before she stole away,
Mama Pansa braided grains of rice into her hair,

tying it with a red cloth.
Later, in the dark hills safe from barking dogs,
she loosened her plaits,
seeds falling like soft rain
into the cupped palms of her children.

II

At the corner of Broad and High there is a wedding.
The grandmother of the bride wears cream chiffon;
she is raising a thin arm, her hand clutching the old rice
                           swept up from her own wedding—
a flick of the wrist, and   sudden as memory

                    rice fills the air

one long grain   resting
on a high cheekbone.

III

Here is your coat of arms:
two and a half cups of rice
one cup of red beans
a dry coconut, a little garlic, a little thyme,
quarter teaspoon black pepper, a few pinches of salt.
No instructions needed.
The secret is in the remembering.

IV

The crows in your back yard don't care
whether spilled rice is brown or white.

They perch on the edge of your roof, waiting
for more.

V

At Half-Way-Tree, a madwoman paces all day,
gently dropping grains of rice into an enamel basin.
The sound, pitter-pat
over
pitter-pat-pat
and over,
reminds her of night rain on a zinc roof.
She is a rainmaker and on a day like today, hot and sticky with memory,
will rain on the queen's parade
if she wants to.

VI

What makes rice wild?

VII

A child sits at the kitchen table picking out bad rice,
her mother singing old-time songs,
savoring them, slowly—
one line, steal away,
then a long pause,
a little salt in the pot,
a light stir,
then another, steal away,
         pause

VIII

In this small zinc house,
we go to bed with bellies fluffed full of white rice
and we all know that the pitter-patter of the rain against our window
is really the swollen finger tips of the forgotten dead
longing

        to come in.

Five

I UP ON TWENTY-EIGHTH cleaning the floor. My mother, your Gran'mamsie, use to say if anybody come to your yard and getting on your last nerve and you want them to leave, you should take a mop and lean it upside down gainst the back door and them will leave in two two's. Sometime up in this place, after I scrub and scrub, back and forth, back and forth, my back so tired I just wish I coulda just rest the mop upside down and have all my pain fly off and leave me. *Over the ocean, over the sea.*

Is thirtieth I reach now. I ride the elevator up and just as the door open and I ready to step out, who I should see but the same work-late man who did try shut me up for singing, fixing his pants and going inside his office. Look at this cigarette he leave burning on the sink. I used to smoke one time, you know, when I was working at the Peacock Lounge. I bet you never know say your Mamsie did smoke, did you? Yes, I used to light up one after the other, there was always some man who would give me a cigarette if I smile nice and ask for it. Lucky Strike. Franklin was never a smoker and he never like it and that's how I stop. You ever notice how Franklin have a head shape just like a question mark? People say if you have a head shape like that, it mean you intelligent. A good-shape head. I wish Franklin would think with his head more and his you-know-what less, but listen to how I running my mouth to this little girl-chile. You wouldn't know bout these things yet, would you?

Your Auntie tell me say I must soon send you bra. But you have anything to go in there yet? Andrea say I have a nice pair of bosom. Funny, but not too many woman tell another woman them kinda things. Maybe is because she don't have any real ones herself and because she know say Franklin have the hots for her; she want reassure me that him really wouldn't go for her anyway, but I shouldn't be telling my little girl-chile these things.

Look at all this hair in the sink; sometimes I have to wonder whether is man, woman, or beast I cleaning up after. I wonder if is so they carry on at home? Can't even wash their hands without water splash up everywhere.

My shift finish and is time to go home. Every time I step out on the street or ride the train, I keep my eye open for Yvette. New York big, and you lucky if you see the same somebody twice, but you never know. Rosemary grow in her Mamsie garden.

Hello my name is Yvette, I'm twenty years old, I'm homeless, and I'm HIV positive. Parsley, sage, rosemary, and thyme. Parsley, sage, rosemary, and thyme. I knew a woman who did name her four children that way. The three boys, Parsley, Sage, and Thyme, and a little girl, Rosemary. I wonder if after all of that, the woman pot did any more sweet?

Parsley, Sage

Rosemary

& Thyme

Six

So Thursday I in the kitchen chopping onion thinking on this and that, when I hear a letter drop through the slot. I pop my head through the kitchen door to take a look and I notice that all the periwinkle have them face swing around the same way—watching the envelope on the ground—their eyes steady looking, just like is a black puss that just drop through the door. I take a deep breath and say to myself, Lord, what going on now? Anyway, I see Eileen handwriting on the envelope and I hurry tear it open, and as soon as I start read what write in the letter, my heart sink all the way down to my belly bottom and I just wish I coulda get swallow up, flush. Eileen write: Gracie pregnant. I say to myself, Alright, Muriel, calm yourself down, make yourself a cup of tea, but you should see how my hands them trembling—all the sugar spill out on the ground. I read the letter again; I must be read it ten times just to make sure, but the handwriting mark plain plain: Gracie pregnant.

How this coulda happen? After me and your father bruck we back and strive to send you money for school, put food in your mouth and clothes on your back, you go off and do a thing like this! Is which bad company teach you to swing your leg them open like that? Eh? Is who the dutty boy? Don't just stand there, answer me! How this coulda happen? How many times I have to tell you no streets of gold in New York!

I bet you the boy is a flea without a dog, don't even have a red cent to his name. Don't just stand there, answer me! If you is woman enough to open your legs, you must be woman enough to answer your mother when she talk to you. Is where that back-answer tongue you did have gone to now? Eh? Look at you, wuthless no-good—just like your father.

Seven

(MY LITTLE GIRL GOING to have a baby. I'll be a grandmother but I not ready to grandmother anybody. Look at Earlie, hardly out of diapers, sleeping over there; how I can manage all this? Only few years ago I was dancing at the Peacock Lounge. I not proud of it, the work did worse than cleaning toilets, but I was young then and I wasn't anybody mother or anybody grandmother. Those days, the only mouth I did have to feed was my own; I could even afford to keel over and die if I wanted to, nobody woulda miss me, nobody did need me. If I was sick and took a night off, plenty girl was always out there happy to take away my job and dance in my place. Some of them did already have two and three baby. It did hard enough trying to feed myself; I did glad I never have no baby. Then as if things never bad enough, I did get pregnant for the boss man. Quick time before it start show, I go country and a woman mix up something and give me to drink, and that's how I throw it away. The boss man never know a thing, and anyway, he never want any botheration, so I know he woulda glad I throw it away.

Now this is a little something between friends, so don't go running your mouth and tell everybody, but guess what? I always had a feeling that Gracie was that same back-answer baby that I did throw away who come back for a second chance. I never tell anybody this feeling because I know say them woulda laugh after me and say is foolishness I talking.

But let me tell you, from the moment I feel how Gracie did kicking so strong inside me, I did know who she is and I say to myself, I keeping this one.

When Gracie born I see how her skin clean and pretty and she fill me up with so much dream. I remember I put her mouth to my breast and I feel how she need me. Nobody never need me like that before, not even Franklin. He was always the kind of man who have his suitcase ready waiting under the bed for his emergency escape. I put her mouth to my breast and I find out say I did have a reason to live. Things was still rough and maybe people coulda say I never have no business having any baby, but every time I hear Gracie screaming out her lungs like bloody murder, I know say she was meant to stay.

After all these years, onion still make my eyes water; now my little girl having a baby, and how she going to manage? I leave her, come to New York; I did fool myself thinking she still a little thing, don't even know bout big woman business yet, but this news drop my heart like an egg on the ground. I can't just sit down and watch my second-chance baby get spoil up like this. This girl chile come from too far. And how can I turn my back on her when she running and crying bloody murder?)

Eight

DON'T JUST STAND THERE, answer me! Who teach you to open your legs to every dog that come sniffing? Eh? Look at you, wuthless no-good. How you could shame me and your father like that? Eh? You think is fairy godmother you have in New York that can fix everything up nice for you? Eh? You think is so life go? What I going to do with you now? You think I can just snap my finger and put you on a plane with a big belly like that? You must be think is Easy Street I living on.

How you coulda do something like this? Such a bright girl; nobody woulda even expect this kinda slackness from you. But look at you now. Good for nothing. Hold up your head and look me in the eye when I'm talking. What you expect me to do with you like this? Eh? Belly big as a jack-fruit. Hold up your head, I said. And answer me! I'm your mother. Where's that back-answer tongue now?

Nine

(MY DAUGHTER RUNNING for her life, screaming bloody murder, but how I can even help her? Is all my fault. I shoulda take better care of my second chance. I was a prostitute in the Peacock Lounge; I not going to hide it any longer. A drowning woman should take good care of a second chance. Now my two hands them tie, and my daughter belly already too far gone for green pineapple. Listen to her calling bloody murder. Murder. Murder. Her little feet them running for her life. How I can even help her?

But look, every time I say that word "murder," a little periwinkle crawl in my navel (I feel it tickling), and look how already they start grow out my vagina—all the flowers them dropping to the floor. So many of them dropping that I have to squat down and let them fall. One by one, the periwinkle balm me. One by one them fall. One by one them balm me. The periwinkle fall on the ground and crawl cross the mat and climb up the wall and rest on the windowsill and listen to the girl them clapping hands in the street. In the street. In the street. Clap clap clap. Murder in the street. Murder.)

· Part Three ·
Tamarind

Andrea

Excerpt from *The Long-Ears Woman's Book of Herbs*

Tamarind *(Tamarindus indica)*
Other Name: Tamara
This large pod-bearing tree from the legume family comes into full season between the months of January and March. During hard times, Tamara will remind you how to make do—roll her fruit in brown sugar to form tamarind balls; preserve her in a jam jar as a spicy chutney. A few leaves sprinkled in your bath will soothe itching.

Advice from One Gardener to Another:

Watch the moon. Know what to plant before moon-full and what to plant after. And always remember: When you hear lizard bawl, that mean rain going to fall.

IT'S BEEN A WHOLE week and still Muriel wondering what to do about her daughter. The bags under her eyes swollen big as nutmegs, and when you talk to her, she just looking off all lost in the distance. I look at Muriel's face, long like the river is dry, and I know it's time for me to speak my piece—I can't keep my secret to myself any longer. My Grans used to say, Besides time and a nice cup of ginger tea, the next best cure for sorrow is a good story.

I remember when I was growing up, we used to sit down on the verandah at night and tell all kinda stories. Grans knew stories that could cure all kinda back ache, belly ache, and pain o' heart; people don't tell that sort anymore. Sometimes I use to sit down and listen to her, and even after the story was over, I use to get a funny feeling that maybe it was still carrying on, and I would start looking around for the ball of fire she just told me about, and I would get all fraid and beg Grannie to let me sleep with her. I use to climb in bed next to Grans and breathe her sheets smelling like eucalyptus; I dreamed fire wheeling by the house, rolling across the grass but not burning it, brushing against the window and on through the trees. In the morning I would wake up fresh as a water lily.

It's a funny thing since I come to this America: Sometimes I don't know where make belief ends and truth begins. In my other life (the one I had back home) I was Muriel's school mate. She doesn't remember me, of course, because it wasn't really me. See, I wasn't always this woman, Andrea . . . but I'm mixing you up, I can tell. Let me start again. This is the story (and it's just between friends, so don't go yapping your mouth to any- and everybody).

Listen . . .

Claudia

LONG TIME I BEEN searching for my mother, looking here and there, wondering who she is. Ida always said not to give up: every woman on this island, dead or alive, is connected to the other like different-shaped beads on a string, even if it's in the way they kiss their teeth or cut their eye or laugh their belly-laugh. Long time I been searching for my mother, and then I find out that my mother has forgotten she's my mother.

Last month, Mother P. spoke to Ida from out the calabash; she was restless and had a few loose ends to tie, and this is what she said: Lucy lives abroad and I'll never find her because she doesn't remember me anymore. This news hit me like a poison rock, I almost choked myself on the guinep I was eating, but Ida pretended not to notice; she just kept carving her calabash around and around with her pen-knife, stopping every now and then to blow away the dust. I stood there watching her hand etching out the twirling patterns. I'd seen her do that so many times before, but this time it was like she had me hypnotized. It was a large calabash, she held it firm between her knees, the carved lines zig zagging in a spiral. My eyes filled with tears, I felt a scream rising into my throat, and the pattern became jumbled.

Lucy

I DID MEET MOTHER P. in the moonshine, under the tamarind tree, just like she tell me. I had my baby in my arms, she was so small—just like

a little doll. I remember I was crying and I didn't want give her my dolly, so I say to her, Please, Ma'm, I not ready yet, let me play with her little bit; and she say, alright, sweetheart, take your time. So I take my little baby outta her blanket and I stretch her out on the ground under the moonshine. I look around and find some stones and I fix the stone them all around her, marking out her little shape, just like how when you in school you take a pencil and draw around your hand or draw around your foot and hang it on the wall. The whole time I there marking her out, I singing and telling joke and making like I happy and she just coo cooing and sucking her thumb and watching the sky. Meanwhile, Mother P. there crouching under the tamarind tree watching me. She did have her own little bundle in her arms and I see her rocking it.

After I finish fix the stones, I pick up the baby and wrap her up nice and lay her to one side, right next to my moonshinedarling that trace out on the ground so pretty and bright. I fill in her shape with more stones and tamarind seed and thing till she shine so bright, you woulda think is sky she drop from. I feel her light making shadow on my face

just like when you see yourself in a river bottom, and then I hear Mother P. call to me from under the tamarind tree and she say, Is what she name? And I say, Claudia. Is Claudia she name.

Mother P.

One time there was a woman that neva have any pickney. People use to call her a mule and the woman neva like that at all. Every day the woman get down on her knees and she pray like Sarah begging for the Lawd's anointing. She pray and she pray and cry long eye-water till her two knee them wear out, but still, she neva get bless. Tings start go from bad to worse, and next ting, she and her husband ketch big fight over it and start fall out. (The husband was a Reverend, you know, so when them quarrel, them did have to keep down them voice and keep it all shush shush because them neva want anybody know them business.)

Anyway, things went on and on, I becoming the mule and Reverend becoming the stallion. I did know long time say him running around with this and that side kick, but I am a sensible woman, and when yu han' in the lion mouth, yu have to tek yu time draw it out, so I come up with my plan and I never tell a living soul what I have up my sleeve; every day I just humming a little song to myself and carrying on like everything smooth, and nobody knew the words to the song except me.

Lucy

AFTER A WHILE Mother P. get up from under the tamarind tree. She was still holding her little bundle in her arms and she come and take away my live baby and give me her dead one that wrap in the bundle. When she hand me the dead baby I start cry, so she take it from me and put it on the ground and stretch it out on top the moonshinedarling that I did make with the stones. The dead baby skin did have a funny yellow color that light up under the sky. Mother P. take out a little plastic bag from out her bosom and she sprinkle a brown powder all around the dead baby and all around the moonshinedarling and then she sneeze three time. She was holding my hand tight and she whisper in my ears, Look how she fit nice. And it was true, the dead baby fit on the stones perfect like the ten commandments. I find myself stroking the baby and singing to her and telling her jokes. I open her eyes and shut them and I hold her two hands and clap them and I laugh and laugh such a long long laugh—the kinda laugh that come from so far, it sound like a scream—and I forget all about my other baby laying behind me sucking her thumb and watching the sky. I don't know how much time pass till Mother P. call to me again from under the tamarind tree and say, Is what she name? And I say, Claudia. Is Claudia she name.

Claudia

I WATCH IDA'S HANDS etching around and around and I remember sitting on the back porch between Mother P.'s knees. She was humming that little tune she liked, the one no one knew the words to except herself. She cornrowed my hair around and around into a spiral with a little point on top. I thought she would never finish, it took so long. She let me get up and pee and drink some water, but then she continued to braid and hum and braid and hum as contented as a sleeping duck. Next day, the children at school said my head big and favor calabash, and I cried and cried and begged Mother P. never to plait my hair like that again.

She just smiled and hummed her tune.

Mother P.

EVERY MULE NEEDS NEW pastures. One day I said to Reverend: Long time I don't go to Antigua and visit my family; my Gran' auntie sick to death and she's the only flesh and blood I have left. I think I should go away and spend a few months. Reverend said, No problem (he was always good in that way, plus he had plenty deacon and deaconess to help him care for the flock). I made him a nice sweet potato pie and packed my bags and left.

Even a mule longs for green grass. In Antigua I took care of business, found a fountain of youth, and proved I wasn't a mule after all. I knew what everyone was thinking: Look at her, she is past the age; she ought to be ashamed. But I couldn't care less, it was the best nine months of my life. The baby was born beautiful but sickly. Three days and she was gone. I wrapped her in a blanket, tucked my tail between my legs, put her body in my suitcase, and left for home.

If someone had asked me what I was doing with this dead chile's body in my suitcase, I would not have had an answer. I just did what my body told me to do. I got off the plane, numb. Took a taxi to town, numb. Got on the bus to country, numb.

• • •

It was evening when the bus arrived. There wasn't nobody much around. It was Wednesday night, and everybody would be either at home or at prayer meeting. That girl Lucy was the only person I saw when I stepped off the bus. She was just standing there, almost like she had been waiting for me or was expecting something. She had a new-born infant in her arms; there were stains on her blouse where her breasts dripped milk. I knew right away I would exchange my dead baby for hers.

Lucy

MOTHER P. DID KNOW long time that plenty man doing it to me because one time she catch me with Reverend behind the schoolhouse. I did see her from over Reverend shoulder, and me and her eyes make four, but he did too busy and never see a thing. Mother P. eye them sad and full with eye-water just like my own because I bet she did know her husband was coming to me and taking his piece whenever he ready. Anyway, Mother P. never say anything and from that time on it was always me and she secret.

I never asked Mother P. where she get the dead baby from; she was the Reverend wife and I did too fraid to ask. I hear say she was spending time in Antigua, so maybe that's where she go and get it. That day when I see Mother P. get off the bus, her eyes did have that same sad look. I didn't have any money, but I did come to wait for the bus to see if I could beg the driver to give me a free ride to town. I never know anything about town, but I find myself with this baby and nobody never want anything to do with me anymore, so I figure I might as well try my chance somewhere else.

Me and Mother P. just stand there with our eyes lock together. I'll never forget it, the baby did start cough up her milk and Mother P. take her from me and rock her and wipe her mouth. Then she say in a little voice, half to me and half to herself: If you only knew what you have. I didn't understand, so I say, Ma'm? And she say, This baby could be your ticket out of hell.

Mother P. said, Strut with your tongue the way you been strutting with your behind. I wasn't sure what she mean by that, but then she teach me what to say and how to say it. For two days, she practice me good until I get it right.

Reverend was scared. He didn't know I did have it in me, threaten-ing to expose him like that. His hands start to shake, his forehead all sweaty; I did hear one time he have a weak heart, and a small part of me did nearly feel sorry for him. Anyway, Mother P. did already warn me, say he woulda try put on a big show, so I look him straight in the eye without as much as a flinch, and I say to him, If you promise to raise and care for her like your owna pickney because that's what she is, my mouth will keep shut, tighter than a dry coconut.

All this time, Mother P. out in the yard humming her tune that nobody know the words to excepting herself.

Mother P.

The little baby lay down on the veran-
dah crying and sucking its thumb and the woman pick it up and start rock
it and hum her tune, the whole time Reverend watching from the doorway,
nodding, truly this is the hand of the Lawd.

Hallelujah,
weeks pass and nobody never claim the baby, and everybody say maybe is
that girl Lucy own, that streggae who did get pregnant only-God-knows-
where and then drop it just like a pup. Hallelujah.

The Lawd works in mysterious ways.

Claudia

THE SCREAM THAT RISES in my throat comes from afar, so far that it turns around and becomes a laugh, loops under, and rushes out as a scream. I am screaming at myself. Screaming at Mother P. At Lucy. At Lucy. At Lucy. Screaming at all of us bending over backways to keep our heads up. Keep the cornmeal turning. Turn it. Turn it. Turn it over, or it might burn.

Andrea

One

IT'S A FUNNY THING since I come to this America, sometimes I don't know where make belief ends and truth begins. Mother P. knew where to pull a few strings and in a couple weeks I had a passport, a visa, and a ticket to New York. When I looked in the passport, I saw a picture of a girl about my age that would almost look like me, but who wasn't me at all, and the name underneath read: Andrea Dobson. I looked at Mother P. wondering what to make of it, and she said, Take it and shut your mouth; your name is Andrea now, and anyway, to them we all look the same.

My grandmother used to tell all sorts of stories about women that change into birds and lizards. One day someone dared to laugh at her, he was a church going man, and it was too much for him to swallow. My grandmother just looked at him and said, I bet you believe Jesus turned the water into wine. My grandmother was a knowing woman; she would have understood how Lucy became Andrea.

An old woman met me at the airport. She was holding a cardboard sign, Andrea D., and when I went to her she flung her arms open and said, Lawd God-a-mighty, just look at my little grans. She cried long long eye-water that streamed down her face and dropped onto mine, and she squeezed me close to her bosom where I could hear her chest wheezing. She said I was her only flesh and blood on the whole face of the earth, and she said she would have to go home right away and write a nice letter to Mother P., thanking her for sending me.

I never did find out who the other Andrea was, but after a while it didn't matter because *I* was Andrea. The old woman fed me and cared for me, just like my own grandmother did before she died. She saw that I didn't like to talk about my life back home and she was content not to press me, so I hid my bag of stones and tamarind seeds underneath the bed, I practiced saying Andrea, Andrea, Andrea, and in a few years the stones and seeds were almost forgotten.

Every now and then, something happens to remind me where I came from. I look at Muriel's face, long as the river is dry; I think of her daughter running running, screaming bloody murder; and I remember Lucy, her belly big with a bag of stones.

Two

I NEVER KNEW MURIEL much; we were just two girls in the same school. I used to sit in front of her, sucking my thumb when Teacher wasn't looking. I was in grade five and too big to be sucking my thumb; Muriel used to look out for me and pinch me if she saw Teacher looking.

For twenty-eight years, I've lived in this America and never saw a living soul who I knew from home, and then one day just like that, I meet Muriel. A friend introduced us: Muriel, meet Andrea. I remembered her right away, she still had that same baby face, and without my thinking, it all snapped back—suddenly I was Lucy. I even recovered my accent, I said, Muriel! Remember me? And in that instant, I scared myself with my own words.

I was relieved when she said, No. I had not been Lucy for years.

For Muriel's birthday, I gave her a necklace. I made the beads myself from seeds and bits of wood. Afterward, we went around scraping up money to buy her a ticket to Jamaica. It was hard walking around all day like two birds pecking at dust, but this is how we did it:

> We stopped at some pawn shops; I pawned my t.v.; Muriel pawned her radio. I pawned my camera; Muriel pawned her wall clock. We stopped at the bank and drew out our little

savings; we borrowed money from the Guinea Lady upstairs; my boss at Safeway gave me some overtime; Muriel found fifty cents in a public telephone; I found five dollars in an old coat pocket; I sold some clothes to the thrift store; Muriel pawned her wedding ring; and just as we were wondering where else to turn, a lady at Muriel's workplace bought a set of her crochet runners. Muriel unfolded the runners and held them up, and the woman exclaimed, "Oh, snowflakes!" And that's when Muriel broke out into such a funny kind of laugh—not a giggle, but a *laugh*. A long long laugh that spun around and around like a thread pushed through the eye of a hurricane. The kind of laugh that has no beginning and no end. The kind of laugh that my grandmother would have said spiders hear, and that lizards and October Pinks flying south know, too. The kind of laugh that comes from so far, it sets fires in its path. The kind of laugh that never dies, never gives up, refuses to disappear, refuses to be quenched. I looked at Muriel and remembered what it means to be a black bird on a zinc roof, laughing at the wind. Outside on the street there were snow flurries coming down all wispy and soft and slow, and that's how Muriel got her ticket to find her daughter, and mine.

After leaving Muriel, I went back to my apartment, and there was a tree growing in my bedroom. It was just a small tree, but a tree nonetheless. The trunk curved out from under the bed, and the tips of the branches almost touched the ceiling. Somehow I wasn't afraid. I closed the door behind me and walked over to take a better look—the leaves were green and feathery, the branches laden with big brown pods. Quickly, I started to crack the pods and eat the sour fruit. I ate and ate until my tongue and the ridge of my lip were sore; the seeds fell all around me, covering the floor. Still, I could not stop eating. I hungered for this sour fruit, and to my surprise each time I pulled off a pod, another grew in its place. Soon the roof of my mouth was so tender, I began to wail. I wailed and wailed, folding myself over into a ball. Nevertheless I kept on eating, as the sour fruit churned in my stomach and the brown seeds lay scattered all around, watching like so many eyes.

My Grans always said, every now and then a little tamarind is useful for a good purging.

Poinciana

Gracie

One

AUNTIE EILEEN KEPT on asking over and over: Who the boy? Who the
boy? Who the boy? I did feel shame and never want to answer her. But
she keep on press me and press me, till I say to her in a small small
voice, Is Overproof do it. Auntie Eileen look at me funny, and she say,
Who? And I say, Overproof, and she say, What kinda name is that?

The thing is Auntie Eileen wouldn't know the man who do it to me.
He used to live in the same yard with me and Muriel and Franklin, and
because he did always keep a small bottle of white rum in his shirt
pocket, people start call him "Rums," and then they get to calling him
"Overproof," and next thing the name stick. Plenty people in our yard
did have a nickname, so that wasn't nothing strange. There was a man
that did name "Black Throat" because him did have a birth mark on his
neck, then there was "Coolie Man" and his wife, "The Holy Cow" (but
only behind her back). And even Tonia mother used to call Tonia
"Barble Dove."

So Auntie Eileen say, Is who this Overproof? Where he come from
with a name like that? But every time I think bout Overproof ramming
his thing inside of me, I feel so shame that I start to sob. Anyway,
Auntie Eileen wouldn't understand. When her school teacher
boyfriend doing it to her, she giggle and sound like she like it. Her
school teacher boyfriend say, Oh Lawd, oh Lawd, oh Lawd, faster and

faster just like a train, and when he finish I hear the two of them laughing. Overproof never say anything like that, the whole time he did
doing it, he just grunt and grunt like he on the toilet. I did want scream
but he hold his hand over my mouth and he press his fingers tight
around my jaw till my head start spin.

Two

CHING. TODAY, A LETTER came in the mail—Muriel coming. All those nights I lay down in bed crying for my Mamsie, and she wouldn't even send for me, much less come back. Now look how I in trouble, and she can't wait to pack her bags and jump on a plane so she can come lash me with her tongue. Is where she find money from all of a sudden just so she can whoop me? Last night I dream say Muriel was a patoo. She had big round eyes that shine in the dark and that follow me everywhere. That part never bother me, but then the patoo let out a screech that send the other birds them flying from out the trees. The screech did so loud, it coulda open the doors to hell; I jump up quick from my sleep and I stay awake the rest of the night.

Ching. Muriel coming, and I feel so shame with my big belly stick out in front of me, I just want to hide. Is all my fault: I let her down, I let everybody down. Look how I did promise Mrs. Cummings to bring the Madam Fate and I never even find it. Now Auntie Eileen say Mrs. Cummings gone from bad to worse and them put her in the Garden. And look how I did promise Auntie Eileen say I would come straight home in the evenings after school. Maybe if I did do what she tell me and wear the training bra properly, instead of using it like a pocket for ripe mango and guava, Overproof wouldn't see me and come chasing me from across the street. I don't want his ugly baby that make from his nastiness. I wish I could throw it away. I wish I did know how to get rid of it. I bet you it will born with a nose spread cross the face, just like his. Every day I will have to look at the ugly face, every day for the rest of my life. Sometimes I feel the baby moving inside me, thrashing like it want kill me. It kick and kick, trying to torment me. Everywhere I go, the big belly go with me. I can't get rid of it, this slimy thing growing inside me. Sometimes I feel it wiggling slippery like an eel, and I wish it woulda just crawl out my mouth and quickly swim away.

Muriel coming, but I don't want her to see me like this. I did want be a florist and buy her nice clothes and lipstick and thing, but all I am is trouble. That's why she had to leave in the first place—too many mouths to feed and not enough to go around. Sometimes I don't know whether this baby feeding off of me or me feeding off of it. We both hate one another. I feel how it kicking and I can tell it have a mind to eat me down to size. But I not ready to give in to Overproof ugly face. Same like how I did kick and scratch when he doing it to me, is same like how I going fight this baby all the way to the end even if it eat me down to skin and bone.

Muriel coming, and I running far away where she can't find me. Maybe I'll go to country, but not to the Bert-them, they'll tell her where I am. All I know is, I'm running. Believe me, I know how Muriel can trace and I don't want feel her tongue lashing my back; the only place she can trace me is back to herself and that hurts like a fire stick. Look how I'm already catching afire; my hair starting to singe, but I'm running.

　I'm running, running. Running through the trees. There's no turning back now. The baby kicking inside me, batta batta like a drum. But that's alright, maybe if I run hard and I run long, it will just drop out; I'll get my flat stomach back, and nobody will stare me down and watch me funny in the street. It's raining and I'm running. My shoes them sticking in the mud, but I'm running. This baby saps my strength and I can't go on much further, but I'm running. Listen to it beating, waiting for me to stumble. But I not falling. I not falling. Is wet and is getting dark, but I not falling. The baby done eat me down to skin and bone, I look like a worm that swallow a chicken egg. We hate one another, but I not falling.

My feet hurt and I have to rest; the fire is just too hot, my clothes are scorched at the hem now. If I can get that far, maybe that woman with all the calabash on her verandah will take me in. She will soothe me with a little mint, and I'll tell her how the story end because I know she waiting to hear how it finish.

See a little dry spot there with some nice white flowers, just like stars. Such pretty pretty flowers, I never seen this kind before. Let me sit right here.

But look at the stars, how they crawling all the way cross my belly. My belly twinkling on and off, on and off, just like a Christmas tree, and the baby laughing inside me, maybe it tickles.

So this is where you grow, Madam. I did think I woulda never find you. Shh, I must be careful how I call your name.

The little flowers mark out a path all the way through the bush. One star after another one. Zig zag. Zig zag. And the whole time the baby kicking and laughing; is the first time I ever hear it laugh like that. The laugh travel quick like a flame up my wind pipe and tickle my throat, and next thing you know, I laughing too. The two of us, me and the baby, walking and laughing, and just as sudden as I start laugh, the baby start cry and I start cry, too. The two of us, me and the baby, walking and crying long long eye-water, long like the rain. The stars marking out a path, straight through the bush. Rain falling, falling, and the two of us no more than skin and bone. Such a long time we been burning up, eating one another.

Three

THE CALABASH WOMAN lay down curl up like a ball on the floor; her eyes open wide but they staring blank like a fish; flies buzzing around her mouth and she have her calabash to her ears. I tap her on the arm but she don't move. I push her harder and the calabash slide to the floor. It have a pattern mark into it that go around and around; it rock from side to side, and then, Oh God, oh God, it stop.

When I grow up I'll be a teacher. No. A florist. I think I'll be a florist. I'll have the loveliest garden for miles around, and my Mamsie, Gracie, will have a different story for every flower in the garden. At night, the flowers will whisper secrets in her ears and in the morning she'll awake as beautiful as a scarlet passion flower.

God-a-mighty, the calabash lay down all quiet on the ground; it have a piece of dry stem on top from where it did get pick from the tree; three words, "spit it out," mark into the side. I watch it little while, the pattern going around and around. My eyes full with water, and sorrow big like a coconut fill up my throat. I want swallow it down but the sorrow too big. I pick up the calabash careful and put it to my ears; a voice whisper, Breathe.

Me and my Mamsie will drink ginger tea and talk to the flowers all day. Bushy ferns will grow from our heads; white moths will flutter from our mouths.

The baby done eat up all my vexation and now it want to get out. This thing them call labor is like when you mad as an ox, your blood boiling hot, and then someone come to you and say in a nice soft voice, Take a deep breath and count to ten. As if it could be as easy as that.

When people come to discover the secret of our garden, we'll just throw back our long necks, our teeth gleaming like cowries, and laugh and laugh.

The red scream that come from my throat, come from far. It leap and spin around and around, then dance back all the way to where it come from; it dive down and travel underneath the sea, it rise up and take in a breath and go under again. The next time it come up for air, it sound like a laugh.

We'll laugh so hard, roots underground will tremble, the shamey macca will spread her leaves, white moths in our mouths will all be released.

Even the wind will notice

pollen falls from my mother's eyes.

Bella

There is a laughter which comes from so far,
only those ears sensitive to high frequency can hear it.

⁓

YESTERDAY, JUST BEFORE I was catching aflame, I gathered all my
strength together and spat. The more I spat the more there was, little
pieces of brown fat coming up into my mouth. I had to be quick
because the fire was upon me, so finally, I made one big heave and it all
came out like a tumor. See, I buried it over there by the river, and look
at the beautiful poinciana tree which grows in its place. At night the
orange-color blossoms burn in the moonlight like tongues of fire, *oh
shali waa, shali mahi wa.*

My daughter's tree is so lovely,
it gives me courage. The wind blows through her blossoms and I am
filled with such sweet fury. I am a ball of fire. That's what I am, and I
am not afraid anymore. When the morning comes I no longer soak in
the river to sap my wounds because the fire can no longer harm me; I
am fire. I burn by day and I burn by night, illuminating, warming, whispering tongues, fiery tongues. Rolling and burning. Rolling and burning. Burning blue, burning yellow, burning red as the edge of a laughter

which can never be quenched.

Rainy season again.